DAMAGE CONTROLLED

DON'T ASK, DON'T TELL
BOOK 3

MISKI HARRIS

FOREWORD

Warning: this book contains adult language and themes, including implied references to violence and sexual acts that some may find offensive. It is intended for mature readers only, of legal age to possess such material in their area.

This book is a work of fiction. All characters, companies, events, and locations are either products of the author's imagination or are used fictitiously. Any resemblance to actual persons, living or dead, places, or events is entirely coincidental and beyond the intent of the author and publisher.

Damage Controlled© Miski Harris 2023
All rights reserved.
No part of this book may be used, reproduced or transmitted in any form or by any means, electronic or mechanical, including photocopying, recording, or by any information storage or retrieval system, without the written

permission of the publisher, except where permitted by law, or in the case of brief quotations embodied in critical articles and reviews.

Author's Note

I spent the last year researching everything I needed to bring this story to life. My biggest struggle was proper use of pronouns and portraying a reality without offending the reader. Please keep this in mind as you read this story.

I wrote Damage Controlled in part as an homage to the real Teddy, a dear friend from my teen years. At that time, just being who she was on the weekend was an invitation to assault, arrest, or death. I like to think she would have a different life today.

Red Deer, Colorado, is a fictitious place which first appeared in the Veterans Affairs series by A.E. Wasp. The characters Ron, Vincent, his husband Kevin, and Benny with his service dog Poochie are characters from that series and appear here with the express permission of A.E. Wasp.

ACKNOWLEDGMENTS

I have so many people to thank for their support and contribution to my Don't Ask, Don't Tell world.

Sandy Bennett: You spent an entire year wading through these words with me. No amount of money will ever be payment enough for the advice and encouragement. You made me able to tell the story that's been in my heart for so long.

A.E. Wasp: You invited me and my characters to Red Deer, Colorado, and we never left. Thank you for allowing Ron, Vincent, Kevin, Benny and Poochie to play with my men. As thanks, I gave Vincent's some renovation to include a large-screen television. I hope they enjoy it.

Kristy: Thank you for sharing your story and your life with me.

To every person struggling with identity, I pray for the day when you are free to live your truth out loud.

Miski

PROLOGUE

Phoenix stormed into her dressing room. Her mood gave new meaning to the phrase "hair on fire" and it had nothing to do with the paprika coloring of her flowing locks.

Known to the outside world as Teddy Washington, Phoenix had succeeded in becoming one of the final three contestants. Her critiques had gotten harder as she advanced in the standings, but as everyone knew in drag contests, a queen was only as good as her last win. Anything could put you at the bottom. Phoenix had won the semi-final round, but the judges' comments had been cruel. Critiques like "It's week nine. Try a wig, we've all seen your hair" and "Girl, you need to pad that ass" were the fuel feeding Teddy's fire.

Fuck them. My locks and tight ass have nothing to do with my charisma, uniqueness, nerve, and talent. That's what got me to the top of this competition without ever being in the bottom two.

Tonight was the finale, and the winner would be crowned before a select audience of VIPs, friends, and loved ones. Final evaluations and scores had been guarded with tighter security than Fort Knox, so all attendees, show staff, and theater employees had been sworn to secrecy. This was attested to in the iron-clad non-disclosure agreements they all signed. There were always the resistant few who couldn't understand why such a shroud was necessary, but they relented when told it was a nonnegotiable condition of admission.

The sponsors had paid major money for television commercial time and placement in the program's ad space and required legal redress against any motormouth looking for their own fifteen minutes of fame. The show was taped for later broadcast, and the world outside the theater walls wouldn't know the results until the finale aired in six weeks.

The prior two weeks had been the worst Teddy had ever spent in any contest or performance since he donned an off-the-rack gown and sang for his first drag audition. He'd been anxious and out of step, and the producers had not been kind.

The bee in his bonnet came to a head the evening after the semi-finals show. Rehearsals for the grand finale were scheduled over two weeks, and Reuben had arrived on the last day of the semifinals. Teddy couldn't wait to get to their hotel room to break the news he'd made it to the finals and invite Reuben to sit front row center for the production.

Traditionally, the family and significant others of the finalists were announced and given a spotlight moment to respond to a question about their loved one and make some statement of love and support.

Instead of praise or congratulations, Reuben announced, yet again, that he had no intention of attending the finale with Teddy's family and friends.

To say Teddy was beyond disappointed was an understatement. "I'm the front runner," he pleaded. "This is important to me."

Reuben pressed into his forehead with his thumb and forefinger, and his voice started out in a tense whisper. "Seriously, Teddy, I don't know why you keep this drag stuff up. You have a full-time job and then you pile on everything for this ridiculous 'hobby.'" Once again, Ruben turned the tables, as was his habit whenever they discussed Teddy's drag career. "When are we supposed to spend time together? I do so much for you, but you're just not grateful."

Teddy knew where this was going. The slow rise in the volume and intensity of Reuben's voice never boded well.

Before Teddy could step out of range, Reuben grabbed him by the arms, and the volume and intensity of his "whisper" increased. "You should be thankful I'm here at all. I'm always the one giving in to your wants to keep us together. But are you? Hell no!! You throw a fit, leave me whenever you don't get your way. But I keep coming for you, don't I?"

He released one arm and grabbed Teddy's ponytail, wrapping it tightly around his hand and causing Teddy to squint in response to the pain. "I gave in on this asinine idea of your mother's to let your hair continue to grow. I even consented to this god-awful color. It's just never enough, is it? Why isn't my love enough for you?"

Teddy remained speechless as his arm and scalp started to sting from Reuben's grip. When Reuben was on a rant, past experience had taught him it was simply best to be silent. History had shown it useless and often futile to counter Reuben's complaints with statements like *you chose the hair color.*

"All the best drag queens have outlandish costumes and seriously over-the-top makeup. You look nothing like them. It's like you're not even fully committed to this thing, and it's obvious you're going to lose. I don't understand why you don't just give this crap up."

Teddy had grown weary of the comparison diatribe. He didn't need Reuben outlining the differences between him and the other contestants and badgering him about quitting. Something had to give. He'd busted his ass in this competition, always believing that, if he won, Reuben would see him for the star he was and finally be proud of him. He'd held on to the unrealistic fantasy of Reuben's toxic behavior changing and their relationship improving long enough. Hope was useless in light of the fact that Reuben wouldn't be in the audience to see when he took his victory walk in all his crowning glory. Hope alone was just no longer enough. Reuben was never going to change.

In the end, Teddy pulled it together. He changed his gown to one which artfully covered the bruised evidence of Reuben's aggression, gave a stellar final performance, and made it to the finale.

The cherry on top of the competition shit sundae came when Peaches 'n Cream learned she'd had to battle Lyza Manwelli for the last spot in the finale. All the contestants were gathered in the dressing room when Peaches, trying to hide the tears behind a false bravado, returned from the stage. She was now one of the bottom two contestants and would have to emerge victorious in a lip-sync battle for the coveted third-place slot. She should have been practicing her last song for the night, but instead, confident she would win the battle and then, through God only knew what miracle, overtake the two leading queens to win the crown, Peaches decided to make Phoenix the target of a venomous attack. With a fury fueled by the harsh criticism of the judges as they announced their decision placing her in the bottom two, she demanded Teddy prove he was a "natural male performer."

"Seriously, bitch, no man has hair or legs like that, and I can't remember ever seeing you shave anything but your armpits. You're just a cheating-ass bitch. You're a trans male, aren't you?! Well, I ain't losing to no ho that's trying to buy what I was born with."

At her last words, Peaches had stormed over to Phoenix and tried to snatch her hair. Unfortunately for Peaches, Phoenix was a much stronger queen than her five-foot-six-inch, 150-pound frame suggested. Within moments, Peaches was on her back, feathers and sequins flying all over the place, Phoenix standing over her with her fists holding Peaches' shredded wig.

"Bitch, if you wanted to get your back dirty, you should have said so. Now look at this mess. Your hair is here, your feathers are there, and sequins are just everywhere." Then, as if she'd just remembered, she added, "Oh damn, girl. Don't you have to lip-sync against Lyza in ten minutes? If you're gonna lose, you should at least try not to look so tacky. Somebody, please give this bitch a brush." Phoenix gave a throaty laugh as she stepped back from Peaches and turned to the rest of the queens in the dressing room.

"Any more of you bitches want to decorate the floor? I am *not* the one you want to fuck with today."

Mumbles of "Nah, sis, we cool" and "Peaches got just what the jealous bitch asked for" filled the air as the contestants went back to getting ready for the finale.

Alaska appeared just as everyone except Phoenix was moving back to the general dressing area to get their stuff organized and pack anything not needed for the finale taping. The space had been rearranged to create a designated area for the finalists. Once the top four were announced, three dressing tables were set up in an area separate from the other contestants who would no longer need the room. The finalists required the additional space to dress for the finale and prepare for the recording of their confessionals. As the leading two, Alaska and Phoenix already had their places assigned. The winner of the last lip-sync battle would take the third space.

Alaska had just completed her taping. She tsk-tsked loudly as she dramatically shook her head in disgust and stepped over a disheveled Peaches, who still lay crying on the floor. After making exaggerated moves like she was avoiding a pile of hot dogshit, Alaska strolled over to Phoenix's area.

"I can't leave your ass alone for a minute. What's this I hear about you mopping the floor with Peaches?"

"She wanted proof of my manhood, so I manhandled the bitch."

"Well, you better move your ass. It's time for your confessional." Alaska sat down in front of her own mirror and began to touch up her makeup for the finale. "You figured out what you're gonna say?"

"Oh, I know all right." Phoenix slid into the fire-colored outfit she'd had made just for this moment. It was her signature look, only on a grander scale. This time, the base of the flaming feathers was made by a magnificent arrangement of blue and white stones. The effect portrayed an increase in the intensity of the heat at its core, which was where Phoenix was situated in the complicated outfit.

"Can you help me with this headpiece?"

Phoenix sat in the chair feeling every bit of the look of fierce determination that met her in the mirror. Alaska set the headpiece and then stepped back to a point where Phoenix could see a concerned gaze reflected back at her.

"Theodore Washington," she hissed. "I don't know what you're up to, but I know that look. You haven't been the same since Paula made that public statement about trans contestants." She spun Phoenix around in the chair. "Whatever you're about to do, girl, just don't."

"Just because you are the one person in the drag universe I allow to call me Theodore, don't get loose with it." Phoenix made a final adjustment to her headdress.

"Listen, in 1969, gay and straight revolutionaries took to the streets in New York City to protest the way gays and lesbians were treated."

Alaska rolled her eyes and placed her hands on her hips in a stance that Phoenix knew meant, *Child, please!*

"I know all about Stonewall. What does that have to do with your confessional?"

Phoenix moved to the full-length mirror and raised her arms, which caused the costume's fiery effect to display. "Well, girl, I'm just saying it's time for another Stonewall uprising, and I'm the bitch to light the flame."

Alaska bowed and smiled, then moved over to Phoenix and put her hands on her shoulders. "I love you, girl, and I hope you win this thing because you are just the bitch to carry us into the new millennium. So, go on with your bad self, Miss Phoenix, and set this motherfucker off."

Head held high, feathers flying behind her like licks of fire, Phoenix moved to do just what she said. Set it off.

If only I felt as brave as I sound.

As Phoenix settled into the confessional box, she considered her reflection in the screen in front of her, then took a shaking deep breath and pressed the record button. This was a one-take moment and Phoenix prayed her words were the right ones.

Hello, I'm The Fiery Phoenix. I know that many of you

are expecting some last-minute sass from me, but today is not that day.

Today, children, school is in session. Over the years, gay, lesbian, bisexual, and all other members of our beautiful community have been struggling for the right to exist in peace. We've come a long way, my darlings, but current events in the world of drag entertainment threaten to set us back. It isn't possible to expect the world to treat us fairly if we are building walls against each other.

In this world, trans men and women have been censored, suppressed, and even punished by the law. And now it has been said that a trans woman shouldn't be allowed to compete in drag contests. Well, bitches, this injustice calls for its own Stonewall moment, just like 1969, and as your new reigning queen, I am just the bitch to set it off.

I am a trans woman and from today forward, my pronouns will forever be she/her as Ms. Washington walks the path of transition to becoming the woman I was always meant to be. I stand with my brothers and sisters in this fight for our rights. The struggle is real, and we are fit for the battle.

PHOENIX RAISED her gloved fist and held the pose until the little red light on the recording screen shut off. If she won tonight, her speech would play as she made her appearance onstage at the reunion and took a celebratory walk down the catwalk as the newly crowned drag star queen. If, by chance, she didn't win, she would have to find a way to make her point in the few minutes given to her as runner-up.

Fuck that noise. Losing just isn't an option.

Instead of the anxiety she expected, a sense of freedom

and release overtook her. It was as if a balloon popped, and all the fear held captive by its colorful latex skin escaped into the surrounding atmosphere. It felt good, but even as she reveled in that moment of joy, she knew her confessional didn't mark an end but instead struck the bell of the beginning.

1

Gregory Grayson's day started out great. It was Friday and also payday, and after his group therapy session at the VA, he'd be free for the weekend. His boss had a major surprise planned for his wife for the upcoming Valentine's Day weekend, so they'd struck a deal: Gregory would get the next two weekends off and then manage the store from Thursday through Monday.

He enjoyed his job at Floors and More Lumber. The work was a little backbreaking, but at the end of the day, he had sense of accomplishment, almost like he'd had in his old Marine Corps days. John Vanhorn was an old Vietnam veteran and made a point of giving returning vets preference whenever he had an opening. There were things John wouldn't let him do because of the risk tied to his traumatic brain injury, but Gregory didn't care. He'd eventually get a service dog and then the world would be a safer place for him.

That was his last thought as his vison turned gray.

When Gregory came to, his first sight was the faces of John and his co-workers staring down at him in concern. He was crestfallen. "Not again," he moaned in despair. "I swear I take my meds like religion, and I had no warning, John, honest." He brought his arm over his eyes to block out the look of worry he knew would be in John's eyes. It was there whenever this happened.

The minute he sat up with the guys' help, he immediately wanted to lie back on the floor.

The area was a mess. Two-by-fours were everywhere. In his fall, he'd hit and unsettled the shelf he was working on as he crumpled to the floor, causing the whole thing to come tumbling down around him.

"You're lucky Lincoln was close by and you didn't hit your head this time, Gregory," John scolded as he and the other workers helped Gregory to his feet. "Come on into my office and lay down for a minute."

Gregory opened his mouth to explain that he was fine, but John shut him up with one look. Frustrated but too shaky on his feet to give much protest, Gregory nodded in agreement and allowed Lawrence, who already had him in hand, to provide him with support down the long hallway to John's office.

As they made their way, Lawrence murmured, "Look, man, if you don't get an answer from the VA soon, maybe you should ask for help from the Disabled Veterans Association."

"I did, and they helped me file my appeal. I'm waiting for an answer now. This shit sucks, man." Gregory stopped walking and took some slow, deep breaths. It wouldn't do him any good to get riled up. Time hadn't been his friend and that sucked, but, as they said in the Marine Corps, you embrace the suck and push through. "They put in two appeals for me. One for the service dog and one to increase my disability rating."

"Well good on you, man," Lawrence said as they reached the door to John's office. "Now get on in there and lie down until you feel better."

Gregory entered the office to find John already seated behind his desk. He didn't remember seeing him pass them in the hallway, but he always thought John moved like a ninja anyway. The look on John's face was grim and Gregory had a feeling he wasn't going to like what he was about to hear. He was right.

"Gregory, this is the third seizure this month. You weren't having them so frequently before. What's going on?"

"I don't know. I'm scheduled to have an MRI next week, but the docs don't want to increase or adjust my meds without first making sure nothing physical has changed." Gregory laid back on the couch and closed his eyes. He had no idea how much time had passed and at this moment, he didn't care. He just wanted to get through this conversation, this day—hell, this week. He was so lost in his own musings he didn't realize that John had continued talking.

"You gotta understand though, Gregory, something's gotta give. This isn't safe—you, or even someone trying to catch you before you hit the floor, could have been seriously hurt."

"What? Sorry, I must have zoned out a little."

John let out a heavy sigh and picked up the phone on his desk. "Yeah, this is John. Please ask Lawrence to finish up what he's doing and come back here."

Wow! Did I pass out again. It can't be time for Lawrence to clock out already.

"You're sending me home for the day? You don't have to make Lawrence clock out. I can just take an Uber home."

" First of all, don't worry, I'm paying you both for the day. What I'm not going to do is leave you at the mercy of some

Uber driver who won't give a damn about you getting home safely. More importantly, Gregory, I'm sending you home for the month. You need to get your health affairs straightened out."

"Please, John, I need this job. I can barely afford my life as it is."

"I realize that, and you're not fired. You're one of my best employees. I have enough business to open a second store closer to where I live, and when I'm ready to start that up, I want you to manage this location, but I need you to be healthy first. So, we're going to call this sick leave with pay. You'll get your base pay every week."

John put his hands up and out, silencing the next thing Gregory started to say. "I realize this isn't the same money you make when you add in the overtime hours, but it's just beyond my financial abilities to pay you all that and also pay the person who's gonna have to come in and do your job temporarily." John moved from behind his desk to the couch and sat next to Gregory. "I know it sucks, man, but you know what we always say in the Corps."

"Embrace the suck and push through." Gregory choked out the words. "I know and I don't blame you. You've got a business to run and believe me, I'm grateful for the paid leave."

At that moment, Lawrence knocked on the doorframe before walking in. "You ready to go, man? I'm all clocked out." He extended a hand to help Gregory stand, then the two men turned to leave the office and head to Lawrence's car.

When they reached the office door, Gregory turned back and gave John a weak smile. "Thanks, John. I can't think of any other boss who would do what you've done."

Nothing could be truer. John always put the health and

welfare of his employees first. He'd made that clear when he first offered Gregory the job, and he was so grateful the man was true to his word.

"Ooorah, Marine. Now go home and get some rest before your meeting."

The ride to Gregory's apartment was uncharacteristically quiet. Gregory didn't feel like talking and Lawrence didn't impose. When they pulled up to his complex, though, Lawrence broke the silence.

"Listen, Greg, I know your health and finances are a huge strain. What can I do to help, man? Because we both know the stress is making your condition worse."

"What I need is for the compensation board to treat me fairly. In the meantime, what I need is food." Gregory opened the car door and moved to step onto the curb, then stopped, shifted back into his seat, and turned to face Lawrence.

"Hey, man, it doesn't make sense for you to go all the way home only to turn around and come back to pick me up for group. Why don't you just hang here? We can eat, relax, then head out when it's time."

"That sounds like a plan because I definitely could eat. I gotta park the car first, though, so make a choice and get your ass in or out."

Gregory gave a wry chuckle. He loved how Lawrence made it easy. "I'll get out. I gotta check my mail anyway."

"Fine, but I don't want you cracking that hard head of yours open, so wait for me in the lobby, okay?"

"Yes, Mom," Gregory said as he entered his building and opened his mailbox. His heart began to beat faster when he saw the letter from the Department of Veterans Affairs. He tore the envelope open and skimmed through the letter until he reached the only section important to him.

Findings:

We have carefully reviewed your medical records. It is our opinion that you qualify for an increase in rating to fifty percent. We further find that your condition can be stabilized with medications and that the use of a service animal fully funded by the Department of Veterans Affairs is not medically necessary.

Gregory slumped against the staircase banister as angry tears began to fall.

Who do I have to kill to get through to the candy asses sitting on these boards?

That's where Lawrence found him when he entered the building. "Greg? Hey, hey. You okay? You didn't have another seizure, did you?" Lawrence's voice cracked as he spoke, the look of worry in his eyes accentuated by the deepening of the lines in his forehead.

"No, this was a stronger kick in the ass," he said as he handed Lawrence the letter and began the trek up the two flights of stairs to his apartment.

Once he got his apartment door unlocked, Gregory immediately headed to the kitchen and pulled out fixings for sandwiches as well as chips and beer. He normally didn't drink alcohol so soon after a seizure, but this day had gone to shit already. One beer couldn't make it worse.

Even if it could, fuck it, I'm having one anyway. I earned it.

Lawrence sat down at the modest little kitchen table just as Gregory handed over the two beers to open. He opened his mouth to speak but Gregory silenced him with a *don't even ask* glare, figuring Lawrence was about to question the drink choice. "I don't know why, but I'm always starving after a seizure," he said, preparing two heroes for him and Lawrence that would make Dagwood take a step back.

"So you read the letter? They just keep finding new ways to fuck me over, huh?"

"Listen, dude, the way I see it, this ain't all bad. They did increase your rating at least, so that allows you some money you can put towards a support animal on your own."

Gregory had just taken a drink from his beer and slammed the bottle on the shaky little table. "No shit, Sherlock. Now from what magic money tree do I shake out the rest?"

"I have no idea, but you know who might? Jordan. Isn't he dating that Ron guy? The one that trains support dogs. You could talk to him about it tonight."

"Jordan!" Gregory huffed. "Now there's a man who got all the breaks."

Jordan, a member of their PTSD support group, had landed on his feet in spite of everything he'd gone through. He was rated one hundred percent disabled after both legs were severely injured in Iraq. Unfortunately, while he was traveling to Red Deer for additional therapy, he'd been hit by a tractor and lost the leg the military had not been able to repair properly.

The VA had paid for a motorized wheelchair and an amazing white shepherd named Deejay as his service dog. Then his friends had taken up money and, combined with his insurance, he was able to purchase his amazing tricked-out truck. Through all this, he also gained the hottest and most eligible bachelor in Red Deer. To say Gregory was a bit jealous was putting it mildly. He couldn't hide his astonishment at Lawrence's suggestion. "Are you crazy? You know Jordan and I ain't even in the friend zone."

"Listen, I'm not suggesting you two go off in a corner and braid each other's hair. Just ask him to put a word in with Ron for you." Lawrence finished off his sandwich and washed it down with the last of his beer. "He's a good guy and I bet if you stopped bitching at him about Deejay like it's his fault you don't have a dog, he'd be more than willing to help."

Gregory got up and cleared away the dishes and empty beer bottles. "Alright, alright. Back off, Mom. I'll ask him tonight after group. Satisfied?"

Lawrence rinsed the plates from the sandwiches and popped them in the dishwasher.

"I'll be satisfied when I see you ask him." He then grabbed the dish towel, wound it, and snapped Gregory on the butt with it. "Now, stop stalling. We're gonna be late."

∽

GREGORY HAD a love-hate relationship with group therapy. The men in the room were a hard-core bunch. If it was round, red, and grew on a tree, they called it an apple. There was zero tolerance for excuses, and they were quick to call bullshit on something someone said if they felt it didn't add up. Thing was, at the end of the day, they represented the one space where he felt safe. These men had his back because they had a shared set of similar experiences. Together, they'd walked one another through some of the deepest and darkest emotional valleys imaginable.

Tonight, Jordan had been pushed by the group into telling everyone about his week when both he and his support dog, Deejay, came in looking wrung out. After a bit of not-so-gentle prodding, he admitted he'd left Ron and moved in with his friend Bishop, also a member of the group, and the guys were giving him a workout.

After ten minutes of the pity session, Gregory'd had all he could take. In his mind, Jordan had the most and whined the most. The discussion had hit a plateau when Jordan announced that he felt his only option was to leave Ron permanently and hopefully find a place for him and Deejay to live. Bishop spoke up to assure Jordan that he had more than enough room for him and his beautiful white shepherd.

That was the final straw for Gregory. There were men in this group, like him, who had real problems that needed to be addressed, and this advice to the lovelorn shit was more than he was willing to handle today.

"Ah, man, you gotta be fucking kidding me. I'm outta here," he said, jumping up out of his chair.

"Jealous much?" snapped Bishop. "Sit yo' angry ass down. You know you ain't going nowhere."

The cacophony of *yeahs* and *that's rights* raised the noise level in the room to unbearable.

"Okay, guys, you know the rule," called out Dr. Mason. "Every man gets his say, but one at a time." He turned to Gregory. "Alright, Gregory, since you're standing, you have the floor."

"I don't know that I would say I'm jealous, but I can't believe this asshole. Most of us would give a nut to have half of what he has. For God's sake—a serious truck, a million-dollar dog, and a hot man who gets you into places with a two-year waiting list? Fuck, you ain't even gotta push your own wheelchair. Just press buttons."

"Yeah, but would you be willing to pay the price he did to have all that? Because it seems to me that the loss of a leg is kinda high," Bishop said.

"Still," said Gregory. "That dude—Ron, right?—doesn't sit in this group every week. He doesn't know what's going on in that thick head of yours. I bet you don't go home every week and say, 'Guess what I talked about in group.' I know without asking that you've never told him how you feel. Sure, you told him about your ex-partner. That shit's easy.

How about the Don't Ask, Don't Tell footlocker and how it really felt when your friend—EJ, was it?—left, and your team members had to report back to duty, and the men in your dorm were shitting on you because they had no idea what you'd been through?"

Bishop interrupted the rant. "That's out of line, man. What does your straight ass know about Don't Ask Don't Tell? Although I still say the gentleman doth protest too much, methinks."

Greg had worked up a full head of steam and, ignoring Bishop, started pacing the circle. He then turned back toward Jordan. "Damn, man. According to your story, you just jetted on the guy, even though he apologized. I mean, everybody acts like an ass sometimes. You just crying here because you want somebody to validate your angry ass, don't you? You even got your dog all nervous. You need to give me that damn dog. I'm still on the begging list for mine."

Jason threw a stuffed puppy at Greg. "Stop whining, motherfucker. Here's your damn dog."

Jason's antic broke the tension in the room. Even Gregory began to laugh as he picked up the cute little stuffy from the floor. "Aww, Jason. I never knew you cared." He cuddled the puppy and, in a poor falsetto, began to mimic a cartoon he'd once seen. "I will care for him and love him forever."

The comedy act caused everyone in the room to scream with laughter. Once they settled back down, Dr. Mason spoke quietly into the room. "I think we've had enough for tonight. Let's wind down and close out."

When the meeting finally ended, Gregory exited the building and found Jordan waiting for him. He sounded unsure as he asked Gregory, "What's the story on you and getting a support dog?"

Gregory saw Lawrence and some of the other group members headed their way. He waved them off.

If Jordan is willing to talk to me after that scene I caused in group, the least I can do is hear him out.

"The problem is that I don't just want a dog. I need a trained service dog. But I don't have the resources, and the VA isn't being as much help as I would like." He paused for a moment. *Say something that may help him realize you're not the prick you were acting like in group.* "Don't get me wrong. I get that they are overrun with a mind-boggling number of cases like mine, vets with PTSD and traumatic brain injury. The problem is, I can't be worried about the VA's problems when I'm struggling to hold down a job that supplements my compensation check enough for me to not have to live on cat food."

Jordan took out his wallet, then removed a business card and handed it to Gregory. "I don't know why Dr. Monroe hasn't said something but talk to Ron. He may be able to help you."

"I love you, man, but sometimes you can be so naïve. You do realize Ron's dogs don't come free or cheap, right? I'm not rated one hundred percent like you. There are limits, and I can't afford to make up the difference."

"Call him. Tell him I gave you his card. Tell him your story. He is particular about his animals, so you better be prepared to attend clinics with him and his staff and show you won't mistreat the dog. Like you said, he ain't cheap, and that allows him to be very picky. It also allows him to be generous. So. Call him."

For the first time since Gregory had his seizure that

morning, he smiled. He held out his hand to Jordan. "Thanks, man. I will."

He turned to leave and then stopped. "You know I'm right about Ron. He's not in these meetings and he doesn't have the same knowledge we all have about the lives we've led. You should talk to him too."

Just then, Bishop and Lawrence walked up. "Are you ladies kissing and making up sometime soon?" Bishop said. "I'm hangry, and I bet Deejay could use some water and a snack."

"Yeah," said Lawrence, grabbing Gregory by the arm. "Let's go get some real food. You've had a long day, Lucy."

2

Gregory didn't know what he expected to see when his cab pulled up to the Pawz with a Cause Training Center, but it wasn't the magnificent stone building standing in front of him. The exterior was so large and grand, he could only imagine what the inside was going to look like.

Well, the reality certainly lives up to the pictures I found online. No wonder it's out here in the boondocks.

Once inside, Gregory couldn't believe his eyes. Just beyond the small reception area was a scene straight out of a Las Vegas hotel. The place could be any urban street in any state. Storefronts of every kind lined cement sidewalks and were so realistic they left Gregory wanting to open the doors and look inside.

"Impressive, isn't it?" The sound of a man's voice from behind him startled Gregory, and he turned so fast that strong arms had to reach out and catch him to prevent a nasty fall on a hard floor. "Whoa there, Marine. That floor can do some serious damage."

"Thanks." Gregory righted himself. "I have an appointment with Ron." He extended his hand to his savior. "My name is Gregory Grayson."

"Good to meet you in person, Gregory. I'm Ron," the man replied, taking Gregory's hand in a firm grip. "Jordan's told me quite a bit about you. I'm sorry I had to keep our conversation so short on the phone, but this can be a very demanding business."

Gregory was confused. The man in front of him was nothing like what he had envisioned. He'd imagined someone younger, more around his age and therefore easier to talk to. The man before him had salt-and-pepper hair, weather-beaten skin, and an attitude that was all business. Although, as Gregory thought about it, this version of Ron owning Pawz with a Cause made much more sense.

Ron indicated a door and a buzzer sounded. "Come on in. You'll see the lower training area on our way to my office. After we talk a bit there, I'll show you the upstairs training area." As they entered the hallway and continued past the glass-enclosed model cityscape, Ron stopped. "This is our newly completed training area. Our service dogs for the blind and deaf are trained here initially. This makes mistakes containable and correctable without injury to the owner or the dog. We provide community service hours for volunteers from the high school to play several roles as we put the dogs through their paces. The kids get a kick out of pretending to be vagrants, stickup artists, well-meaning little old ladies who want to pet the dogs. You get the idea." He led Gregory up the stairs and to the second floor. "But, if my understanding is correct, that's not what you're here to discuss."

Ron steered Gregory around a corner and opened a door to something resembling an arena. It was divided into large cubicles, many of which currently contained a variety of dogs going through what looked like obedience training in rooms resembling the inside of a house. "This is our specified training area."

Gregory caught sight of a young man sitting down on a couch and reaching down to remove the vest and leather harness from a beautiful tan and black German Shepherd. The young man then lay down on the couch. As Gregory stared, mesmerized, the dog went through a doggy door.

Gregory couldn't believe how structured this all was. He didn't know what he expected, but it wasn't as amazing as all this. *No wonder Deejay is so well-behaved.* He watched the dog disappear and he just had to know.

"Where's the dog going?"

"Bathroom." Ron pointed to the vest which now lay on a small table. "When the vest comes off, Ginger knows she's off duty. It's her signal to go outside in her yard, play, and take care of her business."

"So suppose her new owner doesn't have a house with a yard or anything like that." Gregory rubbed his hands across the back of his neck. "I mean, I live in a one-bedroom apartment. No yard, no doggy door, no extras."

Ron smiled. "Relax, Gregory. That's why we work with the owner as well. The young man in the room is Ginger's new master. We bring the new owner and dog together here to fine-tune the training to fit the situation the dog will be living in as much as possible." He gestured toward the make-believe living room. "Michael there is legally blind and will eventually lose his sight altogether. He lives on a cattle ranch, so Ginger will have plenty of room to roam when she is off duty. He has a whistle to call her back when he needs her. When they're at home, he also has plenty of family to assist. Every owner's living situation is different, and we tailor the dog's final training to meet those needs."

He continued walking until they came to a walnut door with a sign that simply said "Ron." "We set that space up based on the situation we're working with, so, for example, when you arrive, the area will look very different."

He opened his office door and, as they entered, indicated a chair for Gregory to sit in, then settled into the seat behind his desk. "Okay, Gregory. Talk to me."

Suddenly, Gregory felt tongue-tied.

I bet he's heard every sad story in the book. No way is he going to find anything special in my little tale of woe.

Gregory rubbed his hands on his jeans. His palms were sweaty, and he hoped the friction would both dry them and diffuse his rising level of anxiety.

"Well, sir, I suffered a traumatic brain injury during deployment, which left me with a barely controllable seizure disorder. I was discharged from the military with a twenty-five percent disability rating. The board said they felt my seizures were under control. In my first year at home, I lost four jobs. The medications I had been prescribed weren't 'controlling' the seizures like the VA insisted, and I don't have an aura that warns me and allows me to get to safety. I then applied for a service dog, but my rating was too low for the VA to fund it. I don't have the money or family support like your client in the training room does. I recently appealed my rating, and the board raised it to fifty percent, but they still feel the seizures will be controllable with the right medication combination." Gregory struggled to not roll his eyes at the memory. "My new rating means they'll give me a better compensation check and they will partially fund a service dog because my neurologist has declared it's medically necessary, but I don't have the kind of funds to afford my co-pay. Jordan says you sometimes help vets in need, so he encouraged me to get in touch with you."

As he explained his situation to Ron, Gregory felt like he was reliving each struggle all over again. He could feel his anxiety level ramping up and knew he needed to take de-escalating measures quickly. He stopped, closed his eyes, and tried to take a calming breath through his nose like his neurologist had taught him. "I'm sorry, I tend to babble when I'm nervous, and this whole thing has me angry and anxious."

Ron smiled and leaned forward on his desk, arms clasped in front of him. "Are you working now?"

"Yes. John over at the Floors and More Warehouse hired me. He makes a point of hiring veterans, especially those of us with disabilities that might prevent us from getting work elsewhere."

"You do know it's against the law to refuse a qualified person employment because they're disabled?"

"Yeah, but since Colorado is an at-will state, all any of my past employers had to say after a seizure or two was 'I'm sorry, this isn't working out' and just like that"—he snapped his fingers to emphasize the point—"I was unemployed."

Ron wrote some notes on a pad. "So you haven't had any seizures since you went to work for John?"

"I've had several. John put me on sick leave for the next month to give me time to get my situation worked out in a way to make it safer for me to work in the warehouse." Gregory rose and started pacing in the small space between the desk and the chair.

"A service dog would provide warning of a coming seizure and, I'm told, even herd me to a safe space before the seizure started."

He stopped pacing and turned to face Ron. "Look, I know there are others in line for a service animal whose conditions are worse than mine, and I'm not insensitive to their needs. I just need a dog that would help me stabilize my day-to-day living. You know, kind of the way Deejay does for Jordan."

A pained look crossed Ron's face but then he seemed to regain control.

Smooth move, Marine. Remind the man of his troubles, why don't you?

Gregory quickly covered his mouth with one hand. "Oh, Ron, I'm sorry. I'm so wrapped up in my troubles, I sometimes forget others have problems too. I didn't mean to bring up a sore subject, and I really hope the best for you guys."

"Whoa there, Trigger." Ron smiled. "I'm fine. Go ahead and sit down and let's get back to you. Do you also have uncontrolled anxiety attacks brought on by PTSD? How do you handle crowds, loud noises? You know what I mean."

Gregory half-sat, half-fell back into his chair. "See, this is the problem I keep having with the compensation board. No matter what my neurologist says, the decision-makers feel that, since my symptoms aren't as bad as others, I don't need the additional help. Someone once told me that the problem is they just weren't prepared to have to provide for so many survivors." He shook his head and let out a snort. "Ain't that a bitch? They were banking on more of us dying! Maybe we should all line up and apologize for the inconvenience of our damned existence."

Ron rose, moved from behind his desk to where Gregory sat and, pulling a small nearby chair with him, settled himself in front of Gregory.

"Listen to me carefully," he said, his earnest look commanding Gregory's attention. "It took a lot of courage and fortitude to bring yourself this far."

Gregory let out another snort, breaking the eye contact

that made him feel like Ron could see down to his soul. "Yeah, right."

"Seriously, Gregory. The streets of this country are full of guys who were not able to push through the suck, as you marines say."

"My friend Lawrence says when you're in the suck, embrace it like a lover 'til it screams your name." He let out a heavy sigh. "Look, I know there are a lot of people out there worse off than me. Thing is, all I can focus on right now is trying to get my immediate needs met. I don't have the bandwidth to thrive because I'm barely surviving." As Greg spoke, he had to struggle to get the words past the lump in his throat. "I just need something to break for me so I can live some semblance of a normal life."

Ron's tone became a bit more professional sounding as he wrote on a pad he'd pulled out of his pocket.

"So, you need a dog that can sense your impending seizures as well as anxiety or PTSD attacks and alert you. Which do you feel you struggle with more, anxiety or seizures?"

"My bigger problem seems to be seizures, in my opinion. The doctors at the VA disagree, but they're not there when I'm writhing and shaking on the floor at work."

"You do realize a support animal won't stop the seizures, right? You'll have to continue working on medications with your neurologist. If your seizures are that frequent, have you considered wearing a helmet at work?"

Gregory could feel the heat rise in his face and figured he must be bright red. "John asked me about doing that. Why does everybody want me to walk around looking like I've had some sort of surgery? The last thing I want to do is draw any more attention to myself than I already do."

Ron's tone as he answered made it clear to Gregory that what he was saying was nonnegotiable.

"The dog isn't invisible. He'll wear a special vest and believe me, brother, that will call attention to you. People will want to pet the dog and ask you questions. Unlike a helmet at work, the dog will not disappear at the end of your workday." Ron's voice had begun to raise, and he took a deep breath before continuing. "Look, I'm not trying to give you a hard time, but you need to understand everything that comes with having a service animal. He's not a stuffed toy that you put on the shelf when you're done playing with him. Just like he takes care of you, you're going to have to be able to take care of him." Ron reached into a drawer, pulled out a pamphlet, and handed it to Gregory.

"Read this. It outlines everything expected of you. You'll have to sign a contract with us, and I warn you, we're not like most training agencies. I am very serious about these animals and their well-being. Quite a few of my dogs are rescues and have already been through more than their share of shitty owners. I will never release a dog to someone I feel isn't ready or willing to accept the responsibilities. So, Gregory, you'll have to work hard and prove to me that you and the dog are compatible and that the dog is in safe hands before that animal goes anywhere with you. This is an absolute must when it comes to my dogs and is not up for negotiation."

Gregory's heart dropped. He needed to fix the negative impression he seemed to be making. *Shit, I need to convince him his dog will be safe with me, or I'm sunk before I start.*

"I promise you. I'll do whatever it takes to keep my dog safe and well cared-for. I'm ready, I swear I am."

"You're still going to have to make sure the dog's health needs are met. Vet bills and food cost money. He's a working animal, not a pet. It's a long road and unfortunately, we won't know you're both ready to go solo until you have a seizure and we see the dog alert. Having a working service dog is like having a love. This means your first assessment will come from the dog we find for you. The two of you must become family, so the dog's response to you starts the process.

Ron leaned back in his chair and crossed his arms. "One final thing. If I find you a dog and I so much as dream it's being mistreated, I will come and get it and you will not be happy with what I do to you as well. Full stop. Your current problems will be child's play compared to the hammer I'll drop on you."

"Sir, if you're able to help me get a dog, I promise that pup will be as pampered as Deejay."

Ron laughed out loud so hard that tears fell. "Please, the world doesn't ever need another dog as pampered as Deejay."

"He may be pampered, but he looks out for his master. I promise you, nobody is messing with Jordan while Deejay is breathing. That dog thinks God created Jordan on the eighth day."

Ron nodded in agreement. "Hold on a minute." He stood, pulled out his cell phone, and waited for his call to connect. "Hey, it's Ron. I'm good. What time do you expect Kevin today? Oh, good. I have someone that needs to see him. Okay, great. See you then."

Gregory started to ask what was going on, but Ron held up his forefinger to signal *one minute* and pressed connect on another call.

"Hey, Benny! You busy this evening? Can you and Poochie meet me down at Vincent's? Great. See you then."

He put the phone back in his pocket and returned his attention to Gregory.

"Let's grab a ride into town. There are some people I want you to meet. I think we can do some things to help improve the quality of your life, and there's no time like the present."

"Where are we going?"

"My favorite watering hole. A place called Vincent's."

3

Vincent's was located on the edge of the small town of Red Deer. While not officially a gay bar, it was known for being a favorite hangout space for the local gay community. The proprietor, Vincent Seton, and his husband Kevin were a very popular couple in town, so it was not unusual to see Kevin stroll in after a long day battling the legal system, disappear into the back, then return dressed in jeans and a tee shirt to happily serve customers at the bar and set up orders for the ones sitting on the outdoor patio.

Over the years, the couple made updates and changes to maintain an enjoyable atmosphere for their regular patrons. The outdoor patio provided a great view of the Rocky Mountains, and at night, the lighting seemed to blend in with the stars, giving off a romantic glow. By contrast, and to keep the restaurant family-friendly, the center of the patio included a dedicated play area so parents could enjoy a cocktail with their friends while keeping an eye on their young ones.

On weekend nights, live music added to the allure of the

patio. The entertainment was usually provided by local bands and ranged in genre from jazz and easy listening to pop hits. There was ample space for dancing should someone feel so inclined. In addition, favorite shows and special events were broadcast daily on their latest addition, a large-screen television inside the main dining area. Tonight's entertainment was the season finale of *Paula Blu's Drag Star*. Luckily, hockey season was over so no battles would ensue over what to watch.

Ron parked his van and led the way through the restaurant to a room in the back behind the bar. Two men were already there, engrossed in a conversation that stopped as Ron and Gregory approached. The older of the two made Gregory think *bear* the minute he saw him. Even while he was sitting, a person could appreciate his six-foot frame that boasted muscles made by hard work. They looked way too natural to come from a gym.

An apricot labradoodle lay at the feet of the younger man, a slender Hispanic man with dark curly hair and a million-dollar smile. The dog looked up, her tail thumping the floor in excited recognition, as Ron led the way into the room.

"Poochie! Are you finally learning a thing or two? How're you doing, precious girl? Is Benny treating you okay?"

The dog stayed put even though she began to whine, clearly wanting to get up and run to greet her friend. The younger man holding her leash unclipped it and uttered the word, "Free." Poochie launched herself at Ron, licking his face and reveling in the full-body scritches. She began sniffing at Ron's pockets, letting out short barks. When she finally settled and sat back on her haunches, Ron reached into his pocket and handed her a treat. "Good girl. I'm so proud of you." Gregory would have sworn the dog sat up even straighter, if that was possible, at receiving the compliment. She then stood, walked back over to the young man's feet, and resumed her position.

"Okay, color me impressed." Gregory moved closer. "Can I pet her?"

"I'm sorry, but no. Ron is the only person allowed to pet Poochie because he was her trainer, and he still tries to teach her something new from time to time." The young man stood and extended a hand to Gregory. "I'm Benny, by the way. This little lady is my service dog, Poochie. When I first got her, everyone used to say she was dumber than a box of rocks. And to be honest, she was—as far as Ron-quality service dogs go. One day Ron had her here for outdoor training, and Poochie came over to me and kept nudging me into a chair. I had a seizure moments later, but for once my head didn't hit the ground. We began working together and over the years, she became the dog you see now."

He reached behind him and pulled out a vest and harness. Poochie immediately got to her feet and stood stock-still in front of her master while Benny put the harness and vest on her. Once she was in uniform, she lay at Benny's feet, seeming to ignore everyone around her, even Ron.

Gregory was absolutely baffled. "Ron, when we walked in here, that dog acted like she was about to pee the floor if she couldn't get to you. Now she's acting like Deejay does at group. I thought you said she failed training."

"Essentially, she did fail," Ron replied. "But she later proved to be an excellent companion for Benny who, like you, has seizures related to a traumatic brain injury."

"Is that why you brought me here? To see Poochie?"

"Well," said the man who'd been talking to Benny when

they first arrived. "I guess that's where those of us in the halleluiah corner who are not cute little furry dogs come in." He stood, extending his hand. "Hey there, I'm Kevin Seton. My husband Vincent and I own this place. I'm a lawyer and, if you agree, I can represent you."

Gregory jumped a little, startled because he'd been so focused on Poochie he'd forgotten there was a second man sitting on the couch. Then his brain caught up with what Kevin said. *Lawyer?*

"Why do I need a lawyer? I'm not in trouble."

"You may not think so, but Benny here was once in your shoes. So was another friend of ours, Troy. Everybody's not walking around with the resources to fight the compensation board and fund the support services they need." Kevin gave Gregory a look that he swore burned a path straight to his soul. "Ron brought you here because what I'm able to provide for you is hope."

Gregory refused to believe this Cinderella shit. "Hope? I've been hoping myself to death. So, what do we do now? Sing *We Shall Overcome* or *Kumbaya*? All this talk is great and Poochie is cute as hell, but this little show-and-tell is getting me nowhere fast."

Kevin shook his head. "What's getting you nowhere is your attitude." Kevin sat back down and clasped his hands between his knees as he leaned forward in his seat. "Look, I know you've had a few bad breaks, but Ron and I are offering you the kind of help you really need. I'm willing to represent you in a new appeal to the compensation and pension board."

"Who said I'm filing an appeal?" To be honest, Gregory was burned out over the whole thing and didn't have the spoons for another round with the compensation board.

"Did you get everything you need from your last board filing?"

"Well, no, but..."

"No buts about it, son. You gave the military a blank check good for everything up to and including your natural life." Kevin rose, walked over to Gregory, put both hands on Gregory's shoulders, and gave him that heat-seeking look again. "You kept your end of the bargain, and they cashed the check. I say it's time for them to deliver on the promise. What do you say?"

Gregory felt like he was at one of those tent meetings where the preacher promised lands of milk and honey while the choir sang *Come to Jesus*. Like any good preacher, Kevin had sparked Gregory's insides, charging him up.

At last! I'm the one getting a break for a change. Damn!

"I say hell yeah, let's do this. Where do we start?"

"A little town called Patchogue, located on Long Island in New York," chimed in Ron. "I just got a call from a small training center there that sometimes refers their tougher dog cases to me." He turned his phone around to show Gregory the video of a medium-sized Portuguese water dog. "His name's River. The center rescued him from a kill shelter, where he was a matted mess."

Gregory stared at the picture. His heart immediately went out to the cute little furball.

Oh my God, look at him! How could anybody be cruel to something so cute? Even if his fur looks like my hair on a bad day.

"I think he's a cute little puppy. He makes you wanna just pick him up, take him home, and prove to him all humans aren't assholes."

Gregory studied the video, playing it over again. "Can something so small be a service dog? I mean, he's no Deejay, but then, I'm no Jordan."

"He is a precious little furball, ain't he? Just don't let his size fool you. I think you'll find River is a bit bigger and a lot stronger in person." Ron returned his phone to his pocket. "Well, we'll see how it works out during the meet-cute. I realize money is a concern for you, but you should know very few veterans have Jordan's resources. River's for certain in your price range. I wouldn't start this if he wasn't."

Oh, Gregory didn't appreciate that remark in front of people who were practically strangers. "How the hell do you know what my price range is?"

Ron chuckled lightly at Greg's outburst. "You know, you really got to work on that attitude. River is in everybody's price range. He's an untrained rescue. That makes him damn near free. For all you know, you and River may not work out, but we'll go get him and the rest is details."

Benny stood up and headed for the door. "As much as I'm enjoying this particular little meet-cute, a new episode of *Drag Star's* is on tonight, so I'm headed to the dining room to cheer Phoenix on."

Gregory perked up. "Oh, man, that's tonight? I'll never make it home in time."

Benny nodded. "Come and join me and Poochie in the main dining room and you can see her strut her stuff on the big screen in high definition."

Gregory walked over to Benny. "The guys in group would give me stick if they could hear me say this, but Phoenix is hot. I'd give anything to meet her. She's definitely the winner."

Benny stopped and turned to Greg his head tilted to one side. "Why is your attraction to a drag queen a secret?" He then put his hand over his mouth. "Oh, are you not gay? I just presumed since you—I mean—Oh, man, I'm sorry. I didn't mean to be rude. If you're in the closet, no one here will out you, and if you're straight, no one cares."

It was Gregory's turn to be embarrassed. "No, no, no, I'm sorry. I'm actually bi, but I just never clarified that in group and I'm always the one getting on people for being ungenuine. Meanwhile, I guess I just let the guys think I'm straight."

"Why? There's no shame in it."

"I know. It's just that I get tired of my whole life being on display. I mean, if I said, 'Let's go to the hockey game next week,' not one person would say, 'Oh, are you straight?'"

"Yeah, that does suck, doesn't it?"

"It does, but right now Drag Race is starting, so let's go get a good seat."

Laughing again, the two men headed out the door and toward the main dining area. Kevin and Ron caught up and the four of them found seating and settled in.

"I say Alaska is gonna take it," said Kevin. "What do you think, Ron?"

Ron smiled like a cat that ate the canary. "Oh, it's Phoenix all the way."

4

Teddy stood in front of her full-length mirror and brushed out her hair. "Mirror, mirror on the wall. Who's the sexiest queen of all?" The beautiful crown given to Phoenix as this year's winner of *Paula Blu's Drag Star* sat in its protective case. Teddy carefully lifted the crown and put it on. "Well, Phoenix, you finally did it and in true fashion brought a firestorm with it."

She considered the fiery locks as they fell softly below her shoulders. As a child and teenager, the kids tried to call her "Red" due to her hair color, but Teddy wasn't having it and the nicknaming stopped. "Thanks to my mom's genes and genius, I no longer have to tolerate scratchy wigs."

When Teddy began wearing her own hair instead of wigs for the drag performances, her mom—Laura Washington, owner of the Mane and Nails Beauty Salon and self-appointed expert on all hair, skin, and nail calamities—pounced. Laura arrived at her apartment on a sunny Saturday morning with a bag full of hair care products. One hour later, Teddy was sitting under a hair dryer letting something called an Omni Pack saturate her hair and scalp using moderate heat. The hair care lesson had taken all day and ended with the application of the leave-in conditioner she was now brushing through her healthy locks.

For the *Drag Star* finale, Laura had suggested changing the color to more of a ginger. "It will add to the look of flame in your headdress." Teddy and Reuben had gone all ten rounds about it the night before, so they'd let Reuben pick from a carefully selected set of dyes. He tapped the one he liked, and Teddy's hair went from auburn to paprika red. Laura had set out six colors with barely discernable differences in shade.

Teddy considered her reflection in the mirror. "Naturally, Reuben now hates the color he chose."

She sighed deeply. "Oh God, Teddy, now you're talking to yourself. Keep this up and some shrink is going to lock you away where you'll no longer be 'a danger to yourself or others.'" Teddy made air quotes in the mirror as she mocked the statement she and her peers often saw written in the referrals for vets who came to them for treatment of their PTSD. She then imagined herself dressed as Phoenix in a gown, heels, and a straitjacket, being led off, kicking and screaming, to a little white van, and broke into a fit of laughter and tears at the same time.

She still had bitter memories of that first psychiatrist visit when a much-younger Teddy had decided on gender-affirming surgery. The evaluation was required by the surgeon, and the doctor's assessment had been damning.

Mr. Washington, I think you're much too confused to make such an irreversible decision. Preferring to dress in women's clothing is not reason enough...

Teddy sniffed. *Well, that was then and now is now. It's time for my truth. I'll be making all the changes when I return from Colorado.*

Sobering, she removed the crown and returned it to its hiding place where it would remain until the show's finale aired in a month or so, then resumed her hair routine.

As she fastened her hair into her signature ponytail, she considered the controversy that had begun to spread throughout the drag community.

An announcement had been made by Paula Blu, the creative genius behind the *Drag Star* competitions, that had created an uproar in the theatrical and political worlds of all things LGBTQ. Paula stated she would not cast a trans woman on the program. Her rationale? "It's one thing to say you're a woman and claim to be transitioning, but it's another thing altogether once you start changing your body."

The drag and trans performers were outraged. LGBTQ activists were incensed and fiercely protested the notion that physical appearance determines gender identity. The entire drag community was enraged as lines for and against Paula's edict were drawn. And it would only get worse when the final show aired announcing Phoenix as the reigning queen for the coming year.

Right now, Teddy's family and her best friend EJ's family were the only people who knew she'd won the crown, but there was still something more that almost no one knew, and she'd run out of time to pull up the big-girl panties and break the news of her decision to those closest to her.

The drive to Chances was quick. She'd been gone for three months, so her schedule would be light for today as she reorganized and got back into the swing of things. After parking in her reserved spot in the lot, she made her way to Dr. Dale Chenault's office, thinking all the while about how the view of the bay from the huge office window would be as breathtaking as ever and never failed to give Teddy a feeling of serenity.

"Well, come on in, Your Majesty!" Dale teased as Teddy walked through the door. "You know, the women in this office want to take your life."

"Oh, really? They still hating on me because my legs are prettier than theirs?"

Dale got up and walked over to give Teddy a huge welcome-back hug. "Nope, it's your hair. Jenna says it's proof that God just isn't fair."

"Oh, God is fair." Teddy pretended to pat down some stray hairs. "Laura Washington, on the other hand? Not so much. She rides herd on this mane as if it were her own."

Dale stood back from Teddy and looked at her in an assessing way from head to foot, his eyes, nose, and mouth scrunched up like he was trying to solve a difficult puzzle.

Teddy let out a nervous laugh. "Something wrong, boss? Why are you looking at me like that?"

"Miss Phoenix, are you wearing makeup? Seriously, your face is as smooth as a baby's bottom, and I ought to know now that EJ and I are on child number two."

Teddy inhaled sharply and grabbed Dale in a tight hug. "Oh my God, the baby came? When? Why didn't you guys call me?"

"Don't try changing the subject with me, Ms. Thing. What's up with your face? When's the last time you shaved? If I didn't know better, I'd swear you were..." Dale suddenly put his hand to his chest, his mouth rounded to an exaggerated *O*.

The grin on Dale's face then spread from ear to ear and would have outshone the sun if they'd been outside. "Theodore Washington, you've started hormone therapy. After all these years. Does EJ know? Does Laura?" Dale then twisted his nose and mouth like he'd just smelled something rancid. "Does Reuben?"

Teddy crossed the floor to her favorite chair in front of Dale's desk in the center of the beautifully appointed room. The old, soft, gray carpeting had been replaced by a dark gray laminate, and Teddy suddenly took great interest in the whorls and circles patterning the wood.

"Boss, please don't start in on me about Reuben. I know you and EJ don't like him."

"What we don't like is the way he treats you. Are you guys even back together again?" Teddy started to answer, but Dale held up his hand and stopped him. "No, let me guess. He was extremely busy on the biggest night of your life and couldn't be there to cheer you on. But now he is so apologetic, and the flowers and gifts are starting to flow like water. Soon, he'll proclaim his undying love and once again, your friends won't be able to see you or find you except when you're at work." As Dale spoke, he moved in front of Teddy and gently lay his hands on her shoulders. He lowered his voice to a placating tone. "You're so smart and so strong in so many ways until it comes to Reuben. This man is toxic, Teddy. He makes every effort to take the bloom off the rose of your success."

Dale's eye's shone with unshed tears. "Everybody who loves you sees this. What we don't get is why the hell you don't."

Teddy shifted her body to cause Dale's hands to drop. She knew Dale was right. Hadn't she thought the same thing after she hit first place and moved on to the finals? Still, she defended Reuben's actions.

"He doesn't separate me from my friends and family. It's just that I've been away so much lately that our time together is precious. He hates we don't get as much as he would like."

Dale began pacing a bit as he counted off on his fingers. "You missed the last two parties at my house because Reuben 'just wanted you all to himself' those nights," he said while making air quotes in the air. "And let's not forget last year at Thanksgiving when he 'surprised you' with alleged last-minute cruise tickets."

"They were nonrefundable, and he got them off a friend who had to save his marriage by going to dinner at his mother-in-law's."

"So, you, an unmarried man, canceled on your family and friends, who had all gathered in one place so we could all have dinner with you, without notice."

"It wasn't really last minute..."

"Teddy, are you high?" Dale walked over to Teddy, grabbed her again by the shoulders, and this time shook her a little. "It was the Sunday before Thanksgiving."

Teddy flinched at the action and Dale released her, moving over to his desk. Rubbing a hand across the back of his neck, he sighed and once again softened his voice as he spoke. "Look, we work with people in these types of relationships every day. It's not lost on me that you flinched when I touched you just now. If you would just listen to yourself and really see things for what they are, you'd see this is a cycle that just keeps repeating."

Dale lowered himself into his chair as he continued to speak. "You guys fight when he pushes you too hard or harms you in some way, and you leave. He comes crawling back, begs forgiveness all while explaining how it's you that makes him this way, but he is a changed man. You take him back. Rinse. Repeat."

Teddy slowly raised her head as she tried without

success to fight the tears filling her eyes and threatening to fall.

"What I'm about to do is going to the end of our relationship for good. I started this during the semifinals but, as you say, he always gives me cooling-off time and then begs me to take him back. Well, not this time. Reuben is not going to take this well, but I can't handle feeling like a stranger in my own skin anymore."

She walked over to Dale's desk and pulled some Kleenex from the ever-present box. "I've weighed the cost, and I'd rather lose Reuben than continue to lose myself." She took a deep breath and returned to her seat. "It's been a long road of on-again, off-again with Reuben, I know. But I realized something while I was away watching everyone's partner support them through the highs and lows of this level of competition—Reuben is never going to be the partner I need because he can't be there to catch me when I fall. In this next phase of my life, I'm likely to fall a lot. I need someone who can take this walk with me, encouraging me as I go."

She swallowed hard as she continued to speak. "Listen, you're the first person I'm saying this out loud to. The hormones were a first step because I've decided to surgically transition. I've been consulting with a surgeon and a medical doctor at a magnificent institute in Colorado." She looked up at her old friend, who'd come back from behind his desk and now sat with one hip perched on the edge of it.

"Dale, do you remember when we first had this conversation almost fifteen years ago now?"

"Of course, I do. That was when you'd started taking drag more seriously but had some confused feelings going on. You asked for a week off to talk to a special psychiatrist your father had found." His voice took on a snarky tone. "I thought it monumental that you would take time off for anything. What's your point?"

"Back then I said I didn't know what I was, but I was certain I wasn't a man. All I could say with any certainty was that being a 'gay man'"—she raised her fingers in air quotes—"wasn't right, but I had no attraction to women at all." Teddy shook her head slowly. "The psychiatrist told me I was confused." She let out a snort. "No shit, Sherlock. I knew that before I went to see him. Three hundred dollars shot to hell."

"Listen, the psychiatrist was an ass, yes, but maybe the time wasn't right for you then. You're much more confident than you were when we first met. Besides, there are better and safer surgical options for you now and, while things still stink socially, the world is starting to make strides forward and allies are coming out of the closet, so to speak. So, when are you going to tell your parents, Reuben, and EJ?"

"I'm gonna stop by Reuben's before meeting my parents for dinner tonight. EJ is another story. He's gonna be pissed at me for not telling him first. We tell each other everything, but this was just something I had to figure out for myself. I only told you first because you already know the backstory and I'm going to need your help explaining all that to EJ."

Dale twisted his mouth to one side. "EJ's your best friend, not your priest. You don't have to confess everything to him immediately. Frankly, I think he'll be fine."

Teddy broke out in a smile. "That's true. Actually, this makes us even if you count the way he came home from the Air Force. So, can we talk about the new little one now?"

Dale proudly pulled out his phone. "Her name is Selina after my grandmother. She entered this world kicking and screaming. I had to come into work, but EJ is still at the hospital with my sister. I can't begin to describe how fortunate we still feel that a family member acted as our surrogate. She's been a great sport, but she told us she hopes we're happy with two because, and I quote, there is no way in hell she's doing this again."

The two friends laughed, then oohed and ahhed over the pictures of the chubby little bundle of joy until Teddy finally rose from her chair.

"I better get to my office and get my schedule together for the week." She moved to the door and then paused, looking back at her boss. "You didn't spill the beans, did you?"

Dale put his hand to chest and feigned shock. "Who me? I'd never." Then he became serious again. "But I want to ask two questions before you leave. Are you changing your name and pronouns now, and when do you plan to tell the staff?"

"I plan the pronoun and name change when I return from the live reunion in Colorado. By then, my parents, EJ, his parents, and our staff will all know."

Dale quirked an eyebrow and asked, "Why do I feel something significant and classically Phoenix is going to happen at the reunion show in Colorado?"

"What makes you ask me a question like that?" Teddy grinned like the Cheshire cat. Nobody knew her better than Dale, not even EJ.

"Oh, because I know you, Ms. Phoenix. You've always had a flare for the dramatic, and I just know in my heart of hearts there's a trick or two hidden in those silk pantyhose."

Teddy fluttered her eyelashes and put one hand to her chest before speaking in a falsetto voice with a Southern accent. "Who, little ole me? Nevah!"

Laughing, Teddy opened the door and was met by *God Save The Queen* blasting from a cellphone held high overhead by Glenn, the building concierge, as her staff lined up on either side of the hallway. Alanna, Teddy's personal assistant, came forward with a tiara and placed it on Teddy's head. She then walked ahead of her, sprinkling artificial rose petals on the floor while everyone clapped, curtseyed, and bowed.

Teddy's laughter poured out. The antics of her staff had been just the pressure release she needed as she walked through the human gauntlet, giving a royal wave to everyone there. When she made it to her office, she found the door had been adorned with a stunning picture of Phoenix in her out-of-flames gown. The winged train extended from the sleeves. When the arms were spread out and Phoenix walked the runway, the entire vision was that of a woman on fire.

Overcome by the outpouring of love from the team, she thanked everyone for the grand gesture and then disappeared inside, closing the door behind her. She removed the tiara to admire the beautiful arrangement of clear and topaz stones. There were blue sapphires at the center of each grouping. Teddy gasped as she realized the settings mimicked the flame effect of her gown from the yet-unseen finale.

Damn, they put serious money and thought into this, but how did they know about my gown...Dale!

She'd needed that little boost from her co-workers and she knew they were the one group that would guard the information that she'd won better than the secret service guarded the president. After all, confidences were their stock in trade. With a smile, she picked up the phone and pressed the intercom button. When Alanna answered, Teddy asked her to order lunch for the team and to make sure Glenn was included.

They'd been great about covering her groups and appointments when she needed to be away for the competition, and the party they held when she made the final cut along with the gift card to House of Zeva gowns had been overwhelming. Now, the only question in her heart was how they would handle the truth when she told them. And she would have to tell them. She couldn't just appear at work one day and say, "*Surprise, guys! Phoenix is here to stay!*" Teddy laughed as she thought of showing up in a skirt and heels. Jenna would explode, screaming her trademark, "God isn't fair," a remark she always used when she attended the local drag brunch.

Telling her boss had been easy because Dale was also a best friend. Dale knew transition was a decision Teddy had been contemplating for a long time and had always been very supportive. Telling her parents would be tight because her father had considered the matter closed fifteen years ago after the declaration from that one psychiatrist he'd taken Teddy to see. Once the furor calmed down and her parents had exhausted themselves reciting their fears for her life and safety because of the negative social climate, they'd support her the way they always had.

Even EJ would be fine. Oh, his nose would be out of joint over his husband Dale not telling him and Teddy holding back something so important, but he'd get over it and end up insisting on holding Teddy's hand through every procedure.

Maybe between Manny, the new baby, and his latest promotion, he'll be too busy to mother me to death.

In the end, all the people in Teddy's inner circle would be supportive. However, she still had two looming problems to resolve: her "I refuse to let this end" ex-boyfriend Reuben and a six-foot-one-inch drag queen slash show host with blonde hair and five-inch heels.

Paula Blu.

Paula was currently trying to backpedal her way out of the harmful statements she'd made about trans women and the art of drag. Ironically, Paula Blu, whose given name was Paul Bloom, preferred she/her pronouns and spent most of her days dressed in female clothing or what she called casual drag. Insider Entertainment featured a candid picture of her taken in a department store. The headline read "The Lady Doth Protest Too Much, Methinks," quoting the line from Shakespeare as the leadoff to a scathing article criticizing her stand on and failure to support the trans community.

Teddy had laughingly intimated to her *Drag Star* roommate Bryan Porter, aka Lyza Manwelli, she'd started taking hormones (just not which kind) after another contestant questioned her makeup choices when out of drag and in the workroom. Another had questions about the length and thickness of Teddy's hair, and the shit hit the fan on the day they discovered that all that hair was, in fact, growing from Teddy's scalp. The wigs and feathers flew as the pointed questions rained down. Peaches 'n Cream led the charge of the small group who seemed to think Teddy was a trans male and wanted proof.

The whole thing ended during semifinals, when Teddy got the best of Peaches and threatened to choke the life out of the next one who touched her body without permission. Lyza ran with the story of the fight to Paula, hoping the revelation would eliminate Phoenix as the front runner. Bryan's actions had made no sense; his scores placed him in the bottom two but still ahead of Peaches and Cream. The judges' critique of his last performance was no more scathing than anyone else's. Further, Liza Manwelli was a better performer and would surely have bested Peaches in the lip-sync battle.

Prior to the semifinals, Paula had made a damning statement condemning the decision of a local drag contest that had announced a trans woman as their winner. She'd vehemently supported the group of losing contestants who'd cried foul. She'd sworn no trans person would compete in, let alone be crowned the winner of *Drag Star*. The backlash from that statement cost Paula supporters and almost caused the show to be canceled.

If Paula had responded to Liza's complaint by outing Teddy as trans, it would have been a career-ender for Paula and a death warrant for the show. LGBTQ+ rule 1: Never, ever out anyone. No exceptions, full stop.

Too bad I beat her to it in that last confessional we all had to make for the reunion after the finale. Live from Colorado, this reunion is going to be a bitch!

Snapping out of her thoughts, she reached for her phone again. There was one more item on her to-do list before she faced her parents. Determined to push through the suck, as her clients would say, she grabbed the headset of her desk phone, dialed the number by heart, and was not surprised to hear an answer on the first ring.

"Hello, Reuben. I need to see you today after work. Will you be home?"

5

As Teddy approached the door to Reuben's house, her stomach clenched hard, which just confirmed that now was the time to do put the final nail in the coffin of this toxic part of her life. Before she could knock on the door, it sprang open to reveal Reuben in the entryway holding a bouquet of roses.

He enveloped Teddy in a hug as he kicked the door shut with his foot. Reuben had a cocky way of behaving when he felt things had come out the way he thought they would. He also never took it well when they didn't.

"Baby, I knew you come back to me in the end," he said as he steered Teddy into the living room. "I'm so sorry you lost, but you have to admit I warned you it would happen." He grabbed Teddy's ponytail just a little too hard. "But now you can cut this ridiculous horse tail and we can plan our move to Seattle."

Teddy gently freed her hair from Reuben's grip and put the flowers on the coffee table. She'd never liked Reuben's place with all its pseudo-opulence.

If only he'd pick a look, it might not be so bad.

Between the French Provincial sofa-and-chairs set and the weird glass-and-metal monstrosities Reuben called coffee and end tables, Teddy had never been sure just *what* to call the style. The one thing she did know was that the horrific Greek-statue lamps and their weirdly yellow lampshades did nothing to add to the atmosphere. Manny had come over with her once when Teddy'd stopped to retrieve her forgotten note-folio. From that day on, Manny had called it the museum house.

Teddy tried not to laugh as that thought came to mind. She didn't want to explain the thought to Reuben.

"Reuben, what makes you think I lost, and what's all this about Seattle? I never had any conversations with you about moving to Washington or any other state."

"Well, you're back before the finale, aren't you? If you'd won, wouldn't they want to keep you on hand for publicity purposes? Of course they would!"

This conversation was getting nowhere fast.

He still didn't answer me about Seattle. Since I won't even be in his life after this, I might as well let that go and try to get this conversation back on track.

"Have you conveniently forgotten? I asked you to come with my family and friends to be in the audience for the taping of the finale. You said you couldn't go because of a work thing. Did you also somehow forget we broke up after that??"

Reuben's voice took on an indignant tone. "So now I'm a liar, Theodore? Let me assure you, I did have a work assignment. You know I'm an indispensable part of our management structure and can't just flit across the country for no good reason, least of all for some overrated drag show."

The conversation was going downhill fast, and Teddy knew she'd have to get it back on track before shit got physical. Reuben could be nasty if he felt like he was losing an argument.

"Reuben, please. I don't want to fight about your job. I know how important you are there, but I have something important to discuss tonight with my parents...and you. I made arrangements for us to meet them at dinner so I could tell everyone at the same time."

"Why can't you just tell me now? You know your parents don't like me, and I don't want to spend your first night back listening to you all argue anyway."

"I want to tell you at the same time because it will affect all of us." Teddy also knew she'd be safer in a public space when she let Reuben know that their relationship was about to end irrevocably. Unfortunately, she was going to need plan B because Reuben's stance and tone said he wasn't going anywhere.

"I'm your man," Reuben replied. "You should just tell me first so when you tell your parents, I'll already know and can be there to support you."

Teddy knew Reuben was lying. The tone whenever he tried to change the truth always reminded Teddy of an old Isuzu car commercial where, when the actor spoke, subtitles would appear saying, *Don't believe him, he's lying.* She also knew she might as well just tell Reuben and go to dinner with her parents alone.

Best to just rip off the band aid in one swoop. So let's just move this convo back to the beginning.

"Reuben, I won. I am the new *Drag Star* Queen. The finale hasn't aired yet, so I'm home until the live reunion show."

Teddy needed to put some space between them, so she rose from the couch, picked up the flowers, and carried them into the equally over-designed kitchen to put into one of the many allegedly crystal vases Reuben kept there.

Reuben followed her. Teddy set a vase filled with water on the stainless-steel counter and began to trim the stems.

"Theodore, you're stalling. If that were your only news, we'd be in bed by now." He reached out and grabbed Teddy's wrist. The pain caused Teddy to wince and drop the knife as well as the rose she had been trimming. Reuben reached out and retrieved the fallen flower.

"Do you know why I always buy you roses?" Not waiting for Teddy to respond, he continued, "They remind me of you, Theodore. Beautiful to look at but hard to hold." He then pressed the prickly stem into Teddy's hand, making his palm bleed. "If you're careless in handling a rose, you'll be cut painfully by its thorns." Pulling a paper towel from the roll on the counter, he dabbed gently at the oozing pinpricks in Teddy's hand.

Teddy stood stock-still, watching Reuben's every move very carefully.

Dale was right. I've not been paying attention to Reuben's idiosyncrasies. How could I have been so stupid all these years? This man is a friggin' sociopath!

Reuben held Teddy's hand in his own and placed a tender kiss in the center, then pressed his thumb down into the palm with enough force to make Teddy wince yet again.

Reuben's eyes narrowed, his jaw was visibly tightening and making his facial features harden as he spoke slowly, enunciating each word through clinched teeth. "Tell me what's going on, Theodore. Now!"

Knowing full well that any further stalling would cause a fight of apocalyptic proportions, Teddy spit it out. "I've decided the time has come for me to fully be myself and transition."

Taking advantage of the sudden relaxation in Reuben's grip, Teddy eased her hand free and increased the distance between them. "I know you remember the first time I considered this. Back then, I let you and my father convince me I hadn't thought it through. But now, I can't continue to live a lie like this, unhappy in my own skin. The more subtle changes I make, the better I feel."

Reuben picked up the knife and moved in a slow-stalking fashion toward Teddy as she moved backward, matching her step for step until he was an arm's reach away.

"Well, if growing your hair is causing this problem, I can fix that for you." He took a step closer, and Teddy took one more back, her back pressing against a cabinet.

"Reuben, I could be bald and that wouldn't change a thing. This is who I am and who I was always meant to be." Teddy kept a watchful eye on Reuben still holding the knife as the distance between them closed.

Reuben's voice continued to be terse and threatening in spite of his words.

"I love you, Theodore. How is my love not enough for you?"

Teddy continued, matching a move back with every one of Reuben's moves forward. "Your love has always been more than enough. It's the way you demonstrate that love that gives me pause."

I am not going to let him cut my hair or me. I'm out of here once I round this counter.

"See, this is exactly what I'm always telling you, Teddy. You're ungrateful and uncaring. I give you every damn thing I am, and it's still not enough."

Reuben was so enraged he didn't realize the knife had moved in his hand. When he once again tightened his grip, the blade pierced his skin. "Fuck!" he screamed as he dropped the knife to the floor. "Look what you made me do! You know what? You're right. You're not worthy of my love and affection. You think I need you?! Well, I don't. Get out of my house and get out of my life, bitch."

Laura Washington's daughter did NOT need to be told twice. Teddy didn't waste a single moment getting through the hall and out the door. She was in her car and safely starting it when Reuben came through the door with the knife in his hand and screaming like a maniac. Heart pounding, she pulled out of the driveway and headed to the Sayville Inn to meet her parents.

Damn, that could've gone better. I'm not sure how, but it could. I've been such an idiot not to realize it could come to this. I'm going to be keeping my eyes wide open until I leave for Colorado.

6

The Sayville Inn was originally a small tavern and had been a fixture in historic Sayville since 1888. It had expanded over the centuries and now featured an impressive taproom and restaurant. The number of work-related meetings, trainings, and family dinners Teddy had attended here in her lifetime were too numerous to count. This was the place where the Washington family had gone for dinner when a fourteen-year-old Teddy had explained to his parents that he didn't then, nor would he ever, like or date girls.

"How do you know?" his father had asked. "Have you even tried?"

Laura came to the rescue for what would be the first of many times. "Nathan," she had said, "how many men did you date before you were sure that women were it for you in general and me in particular?" Her voice was dangerously soft, and the conversation ended without further protest from his father.

Taking a deep breath and shaking off her walk down memory lane, Teddy entered the restaurant and was led to one of the small private dining rooms. This was another reason he loved the Sayville Inn. Their policy that no group was too small for a private setting was perfect for the conversation about to take place. She gave a nod to Gordon, the evening manager, whom she knew all too well.

"Did they order drinks yet, Gordon?"

"Oh, is it gonna be that kind of night, then? I'll get your father's favorite Scotch and your mom's favorite wine out and at the table right away. Which of your many favorites are you having?"

"Long Island Iced Tea. Make it strong."

"Damn, Teddy, who'd you kill? Or are you the one about to die?"

"Ironically, Gordon, some may think it's both."

Gordon moved quickly into the taproom and reemerged with a rolling cart. Together, he and Teddy walked into the small room where her mother and father sat talking quietly.

"Sorry I'm late, guys. I had to handle a personal matter first." Teddy walked over to kiss her mother on the cheek. "I did bring the drink service with me." She indicated Gordon, who was busy setting drinks and water on the table. Once he had finished, Gordon gave them all a slight nod before he left the room, saying, "Your waiter will be right in to take your orders."

Laura made an exaggerated show of taking a sip of her wine before starting in on the elephant in the room. "So, how unhappy is Reuben today? Is it the length of your hair, the new color—which he chose, by the way—or is he having a true hissy fit because you won?"

"All of the above, Mom. We also broke up," Teddy answered as she moved to shake hands with her father.

Nathan kept his hold on Teddy, his eyebrows raised high. "What the hell happened to your wrist? And don't bullshit me, boy, because we both know you couldn't tell a believable lie if your life depended on it."

In her haste to get away from Reuben and to the restaurant on time, Teddy had failed to notice the bruise forming where Reuben had grabbed her. Sure enough, a distinct, swollen lesion was noticeably purpling against her fair skin.

"Reuben grabbed my arm." Teddy smiled slightly to lighten the tension a bit. "He wasn't, shall we say, extremely receptive to anything I had to say. I'm alright though, and Reuben and I are finished for good." She looked her father in the eye. "Look at my face, Dad. You're right, I've never been able to lie to you. So trust me when I say I'm really good for the first time in years. And that includes me realizing I needed to eliminate Reuben from my life forever." Teddy quickly sat down, picked up her Long Island Iced Tea, and took a deep drink from the strong brew.

Nathan Washington pulled a roll from the basket in the center of the table, split it in half, and slowly applied butter to it, all the while watching his only child gulp her drink. At last, he said, "Okay. Theodore. I know you didn't bring us here to announce your breakup with the Vampire Lestat, so spill it, son."

Laura Walker wasn't having it. "Nathan, I want the two of you to stop trying to play this down like it was nothing. We just got here, and I, for one, want to know what led Reuben to assault my son. Do we need to call the police? I mean, there are laws against this kind of thing."

"Mom, please calm down. Reuben is handled, and I am taking this seriously. If he tries anything else, which I doubt, I promise to involve the police. In the meantime, I am really starving, and I have a lot to say, so can we at least start dinner before the Washington family inquisition begins?"

Laura finally smiled at Teddy. "Well, at least I'm glad to

see you're adhering to that regimen I taught you, honey. Your hair is handling all that stiffening spray abuse well. It looks healthy and it's so long. Are you going to cut it at all?"

"No, Mom, but I will let you trim the edges. I know that's what's coming next." Teddy had to admit she loved the way her mom fussed over her.

In short order, their food arrived, and conversation stopped except for "This is good!" and the occasional "Pass the salt." And Laura chiding Nathan with, "Don't forget what the doctor said about salt and your blood pressure."

Soon enough, dessert and coffee were on the table, and Teddy knew the time had come.

"So." She paused for a second and cleared her throat. "As you know, I won the crown on *Drag Star*."

"We were there, boy. Spill." Nathan made it clear that the drag-it-out approach was not appreciated.

"Well, next month all the contestants will be appearing live in Colorado for a reunion show. It's scheduled to air one week after the finale." Teddy pulled the band out of her ponytail. This was the hard part. "Um, well..." She paused to mentally brace herself. "The three finalists did these confessional pieces, so in about five weeks the world is going to hear me declare I'm trans female and have begun treatment in preparation for gender-affirming surgery."

Teddy spit the words out so fast she wasn't sure that even she understood what she said. Steeling for the fallout, she pulled her coffee cup close and concentrated on stirring sugar into the steaming black drink.

Teddy's mother reached across the table, placed her fingers under Teddy's chin, and slowly lifted her head up so they were facing each other eye-to-eye. The concern on her face broke Teddy's heart. Just once, she wanted to make an announcement to her parents that made joy their first response.

"Is that what this dinner is all about?" she said slowly. "You want us to know you've decided to move forward with your transition?" She made a quiet tsking sound through her teeth. "Child, you could have saved yourself some money. I already knew that was coming, so hold your head up. Ain't no answers in that coffee cup." Laura sat back in her seat and topped off her coffee from the carafe on the table. "Why do you think I've been riding herd on you about your hair? I knew by the time you figured it all out, your hair would be an irretrievable hot mess if I didn't. Everybody knows a black woman's crowning glory is her hair."

"Laura, are you listening to yourself? My son just announced he is now my daughter, and you want to talk about hairstyles?" Nathan threw his napkin on the table. "Now look, Teddy. I went with you to that psychiatrist the first time you tried this. He said you were wrong."

"No, Dad, that's not what he said. He said I was confused and, in my state at the time, should not make such a life-altering decision. Back then, I was just beginning to understand who I was inside." Teddy blew out a hard breath of exasperation through her nose. She needed her father to realize the difference between Teddy and Phoenix. More importantly, she needed him to see this wasn't some sort of phase. Her life was about to change permanently, and she needed her father in her corner now more than ever.

"That was then, Dad, now is now. I'm not confused. I've spent all my adult life trying to live as two people, but I just can't do that anymore. It's time for me to be one hundred percent about who I am inside."

Tears threatened to fall from Nathan's eyes, and it just about broke Teddy.

"Teddy, I love you, and I'll love you no matter how you look or what you call yourself. But I want to make sure you understand the side effects are not just from surgery, son. This world is on a rampage against trans men and women. When I was a kid, it was criminal to be gay. In some states, it still is." Nathan stopped to take a sip of his coffee and Teddy noticed his hand shake slightly, a leftover symptom from a prior neurological illness and a clear indication of her father's level of anxiety.

"You young people talk about Stonewall, but I was there that day. Your mom and I were at the Purple Onion for a Grover Washington set. When the police raided the Stonewall Inn, all hell broke loose in the Village. The police were unprepared, and the mafia owners were angry because they'd been paying graft money for years to prevent this kind of thing from happening. Passersby and neighborhood residents began to raise hell with the police. The response was epic."

His hands flew as he tried to emphasize his words. His voice had begun to get louder and when Laura signaled him to lower his volume, he took a deep breath and spoke in a slower, quieter tone.

"People died, Teddy. It was illegal to be homosexual in New York, and those men and women took their lives in their hands every time they left home." Nathan wiped his eyes with his napkin, then got out of his chair and walked over to where Teddy sat, taking the empty chair next to her.

"Your mother and I have watched you struggle with this for years. I know it's selfish, but I just kept praying you would choose to stay my son. Not because I'd be ashamed of you, but because I'm so fucking afraid for you."

Teddy couldn't hold back the tears anymore. Her mother was her heart, but her father was her soul. "I always wondered why you never stayed in the military until retirement. I think I know though. You'd never stand by and see someone wrongfully treated."

"As a black man, it was hard enough being in the military, but to stand by and watch a brother marine get beaten to within an inch of his life because of who he chose to love and then receive a dishonorable discharge while he was in the hospital was more than I was willing to tolerate. But enough about my past. We're discussing your future."

Nathan returned to his seat and freshened his coffee. "So, what's next, Teddy? Tell us about this statement you made."

Teddy carefully recited the statement she had made in the confessional for her parents. As she spoke, she noticed a look of determination cross her mother's face that she'd not seen since she came out to her parents as a teenager. Her father, on the other hand, looked confused.

"I don't understand, Teddy. That sounds more like a declaration of war than a gender announcement."

"Oh, Nathan. I sometimes forget you don't read the tabloid news." Laura set her cup on the table.

Strap in, folks. Mom's about to take off.

"That Paula creature made a statement that she wouldn't allow a trans woman to compete on *Drag Star*. Teddy's confessional statement draws a line in the sand and, frankly, *is* a declaration of war." The expression on her face morphed into one of concern as she stopped speaking and put her hand to her mouth. "Oh no, Phoenix! Does that mean the evil bitch is going to take your crown? Because if she does, I'll kick her ass for you. Nobody messes with my baby."

Nathan massaged his temples with an intensity that

looked like he was going to break the skin. "This. This is what I'm talking about, Theodore."

Here it comes. All hell is about to break loose.

"Look. This woman was making a stink long before you won and decided to publicly defy, not to mention embarrass, her. Speaking of which, what in the hell were you thinking? I'm guessing maybe you thought you were going to make some great strike for all trans-kind, but that's not going to happen."

Nathan held up one hand and Teddy knew the countdown was about to commence.

Tapping each finger as he spoke, Nathan laid out his thoughts. "First. It's not going to be a surprise for Paula on that day. Frankly, before she allows something to air that will embarrass them, that segment of the show will wind up on the cutting floor. Those confessionals were pre-recorded, so something else can easily be used to fill in. They can substitute video of your performances in the competition, for example. Second. That crown you're so proud of can be rescinded. And before you say you'll refuse to send it back, know that they have at least a dozen of them and can crown a new queen at the reunion without you, who will by then have been uninvited. Third. They have teams of people who know how to spin shit like this. Fourth—"

Laura grabbed her husband's hands and interjected, "I think you've made your point, sweetheart."

Nathan pulled his hands away gently but firmly. "No, I haven't. Teddy, have you considered the fact that you're a public figure and will set yourself up for physical harm from crazy people who think you have no right to be a woman? Some of whom may be clients in the very clinic you work in."

"Our clients already know I'm a drag queen, Dad."

"Don't play dumb with me, Theodore. We aren't talking about drag. We're talking about your life. Something very precious that I don't want you to lose."

Laura spoke up in agreement. "Your father is right in this regard. Why can't this part of your life be private? Why does the world have to know? What you've done is dangerous and we just want you to consider the cost. I know you, and I know there was a reason in your head for what you did. But you're about to turn the most important decision you've ever made into a dumpster fire instead of a cause for celebration."

Teddy walked over to the little cart that held the wine her mother had been drinking with dinner and poured herself a glass.

I need this more than I need coffee.

"The other queens were giving me stick about my hair, how I never seemed to have to shave my legs, the lack of five o'clock shadow, my makeup, you name it. One even wanted to touch my penis to see if it was real." Teddy let out a short huff. "They thought I was trans male. My roommate saw me taking my meds and asked about it. I told him they were hormones and laughed when I said it, as if I was joking. He ran to Paula who asked me point-blank if I was male or female."

Nathan shook one finger at Teddy. "This is exactly what I was talking about. What did you tell her?"

"I said I didn't know. So, she told me to figure it the fuck out before the finale or she'd kick my front-runner ass right off her show."

Nathan started to speak but Teddy held up a hand to stop him.

"There's more. A trans woman won a local drag contest, and it made the news. Naturally, they interviewed Paula as host of the national competition. That's when she made that damning statement. I took it as a veiled threat and so when my turn came in the confessional box, I drew my line in the sand."

Nathan shook his head. "I love you. You're one of the smartest people I know, but sometimes you act like you don't have the common sense God gave a billy goat. Always leading with your chin. Why?"

"I don't know, Dad. Until now, my biggest concern was letting the people I love know my decision. As usual, you two have brought up consequences I'd not given serious thought to."

"Well, the drag's outta the bag now. Colorado's next month. You may have less time than that, depending on Paula, so you better figure it out," Laura said as she signaled for the check.

"I've got this one, son. What you're about to do is expensive to do right. You're gonna need every dime you can save."

"Thanks, Mom. You guys are the best."

"Not a problem. We'll drop you off at home though. You've had more than your usual limit. You can just walk over and pick up your car tomorrow."

The ride home was quiet. Teddy's thoughts were focused on the conversation she'd had with her parents. They'd made some valid points.

Dad's right. I led with my chin. I was only thinking about the negative impact of Paula's statement on trans men and women who want to begin or continue to participate in the drag entertainment field.

The contest was one thing, but life after the reunion show could be a horse of a different color. She hadn't just put his crown on the line. She'd just thrown his entire life into the ring.

Well, it is what it is. I meant what I said, so I'm just going to have to find a way to embrace the suck, as my clients say.

Teddy bid her parents goodbye as she exited the car. Her jaunt to her apartment door slowed as she spotted a glass vase filled with roses. Resting in the bed of flowers lay a note.

Theodore,

I don't know what got into me. Forgive me, please. We can work this out.

I love you with everything I am.

Reuben

She entered her apartment and set the vase on the little hall table where she kept his keys and threw her mail.

I should have known it wouldn't be that simple.

Teddy still had one major hurdle to cross that was going to make everything else seem like child's play.

Ending it for good with Reuben.

7

When Ron and Gregory deplaned at MacArthur Airport, Gregory was surprised to find so much crammed into the compact space. He knew it was a local airfield and expected it to be small, but it was miniature compared to Denver International. Because of its size, he was amazed to learn four major airlines had hubs there. In addition, it had all the trappings of any other major air station. Bars, restaurants, and gift shops greeted him along the short walk to baggage claim and the car rental area. There was even a TGI Fridays and a Starbucks.

By comparison, the airport in Denver had been a virtual city in itself. Gregory couldn't help but think they were going to need to flag down one of those motor cars to make it to their gate without passing out. He had kept shifting his duffle from left to right as they traversed the cavernous place.

"Thank God for the training the Corps gave me."

Ron had laughed. "What's the matter, Marine? You out of shape?"

"It is kind of a hike, man. Why didn't we just park on the other side?"

"Okay, traveling with animals 101," said Ron. "When we get back, we may have River. Since he won't be certified yet, we'll have to send him as cargo. By the time we get him off the plane and out of the shipping area, it will be prudent to get him out of the airport as quickly as possible."

Now, as they made the short jaunt to the car rental desk, Gregory felt fortunate they'd not checked any bags. It was just a matter of picking up their car and hitting the road.

The hustle and bustle of the crowd that began to form around the baggage claim belts began to spread over into the small car rental area. He was starting to feel a bit anxious and all but sprinted through the exit door to the cool afternoon air where he waited for Ron while he pulled himself together.

After a fifteen-minute drive, they parked in the private lot for the Patchogue Training Center. They were met by Leroy Dumphrees, the center's director.

"Ron! It's good to see you again." He turned to Gregory. "This is your client, I presume." He stepped forward and held out his hand. "Hey, I'm Leroy and I hope you're Gregory."

Gregory couldn't help but laugh at the rotund, gray-haired man. *If his hair and beard were white, he'd be the perfect Santa Claus at Christmas time.*

Gregory reached out and shook Leroy's hand. "Pleased to meet you." *Did his eyes just twinkle?*

Leroy let out a hearty laugh. "I know exactly what you're thinking. I remind you of Santa Claus, am I right?"

Gregory face felt hot, and he knew that, even with his skin tone, Ron and Leroy could tell he was blushing.

Damn, can he read my mind?

Ron clapped Gregory on the back. "Don't worry, Gregory, you aren't the first. And Leroy here does play Santa Claus for the Sayville Holiday Fest, the annual parade, and the tree lighting every year. Don't get me started on how he decorates his house."

"It's my pride and joy," Leroy said. "The money I raise from the donations each year support cancer treatment and research for children." He clapped his hands together. "Well, enough about me, let's go meet the pup of the hour." He led Ron and Gregory through a nearby door and down a hallway to the kennel area. In the last of a row of empty cages, a little black ball of fur lay curled up sleeping. Larry walked to the gate and called out to the roll of fluff. "River, come say hello." The furball came alive and ran for the gate, tail wagging a mile a minute. "You want to come out and meet Gregory?" He opened the gate and River bounded out, clearly happy to be free of the confined space.

Gregory looked down at the cute pup. "I bet you're happy to be out of there, aren't you, boy?" He wanted to stoop down and meet the cute little dog, but he couldn't shake the feeling of being overwhelmed. He wasn't prepared for all the tight spaces. He'd expected the training center to be similar in scope to Pawz for a Cause. Instead, it was only one story and maybe half the overall size. He wasn't a fan of the feeling that everything was closing in on him.

First the plane, then the airport, and now this place. It's gonna be a long week.

Ron walked over to him, and a look of worry crossed his face. "You okay? You look like you're going to pass out."

As Ron spoke, River ran over to Gregory, barking and nudging him with his head.

Gregory had started to sweat. "I'm good. I just need some..."

Before he could get the words out of his mouth, Ron lowered him to the floor. When he came to, he was lying on the floor, his head in Ron's lap. Ron and Larry slowly helped him sit up and guided him into a chair he didn't remember seeing before. River was back in the kennel, pacing back and forth in front of the gate.

"Did I seize? I don't feel postictal." Stressed and confused, he held his head with both hands. Ron pressed a cold bottle of water into his hand. Gregory took it gratefully and drank deeply, the cool liquid comforting his throat, which felt dry and scratchy, like desert sand.

"Slow down," Ron chided. "Give your body time to recover. You didn't have a seizure. It looks more like you had an anxiety attack."

"I haven't had one of those in ages." He patted his pockets and pulled out an amber pill bottle, then shook out a pill and swallowed it with the remainder of his water. He looked toward the cage at the pacing dog. "Is River okay? I didn't fall on him or anything, did I?"

Ron smiled as Leroy moved over to the gate and set the little fluff ball free.

"River is better than you know. We had only one aspect that concerned us about him. Portuguese water dogs are known to be very sensitive to human emotion, but River gave us no sign that he held such instincts until now. His alert gave us time to keep you safe, so I feel confident in bringing him home to train with you."

River bounded over to Gregory, happily dancing around his feet.

Gregory ran his hands through the curly fur. "Well, he certainly seems to like me. His fur feels funny though. It's soft and curly, more like hair." He looked at the little feet resting on his knees. Shocked at what he saw, he picked up one paw to examine it more closely "And what's wrong with his paws? They look odd."

Leroy laughed. "When we first saw River, we thought it was impossible that he was a purebred because his is a very expensive breed. Portuguese water dog puppies go for upwards of two thousand dollars. No way he should be in a shelter. We rescued him, cleaned him up, and had him tested. It turns out he is one hundred percent purebred and was abandoned by an idiot."

Gregory slowly put the cute dog down. He was so crestfallen he couldn't even hear Leroy's explanation of the dog's strange features.

No way in hell, even with Ron's generosity, can I afford a dog like that. Damn him for setting me up like this!

"Gregory?" Leroy asked. "Something wrong, son?"

Ron spoke up. "Gregory, he's still a rescue. Two thousand dollars isn't his price, it's simply his value. That curly mop is hair. His feet are webbed because these dogs are amazing swimmers and hunters."

"Exactly how much is this dog going to cost me? Don't get my hopes up. I've had enough disappointment to last me a lifetime."

"Let's get River back to Red Deer and see how you two work out first. He seems to have potential to be what you need if his actions when you had your panic attack are anything to go by. I wouldn't have brought you with me if I didn't think we could make this work and that you'd meet the first of my requirements."

Gregory was shocked. He'd never considered the possibility Ron would turn him down for any reason other than money. "You've denied people before? Why?"

Larry spoke up. "Ron and I are different from many trainers. Money isn't enough to get one of our dogs." He reached down and snapped a leash on River, then handed the lead to Gregory. "Come with me." He led Gregory and River to a different room. It was large and lit up like a sunny day, with kennels lining the perimeter.

"This is where we bring the rescues. We groom them, catch up their shots, and begin their testing and training." He walked over to River and took the lead from Gregory, then gave River a series of simple dog-training commands. As Gregory watched, he found himself cheering inside each time River promptly obeyed.

"So, what makes River not acceptable for your clients? He seems pretty damn smart to me." River looked up at him as if he knew Gregory was talking about him. He then gently placed his paws on Gregory's knees, and something in the soulful eyes made Gregory's heart melt.

"I love him already. At this point, I'd sell a kidney to take him home."

"Oh, I never said I couldn't potentially use River. I know that Ron has access to more traumatic brain injury clients than I do because of his tie-in with the VA, so when I get one like River, which isn't often, I call him first."

Gregory's question still wasn't answered. "So how do people qualify with your two?"

Ron had been leaning against a wall all this time watching Gregory, River, and Larry interact. He slowly pulled himself away from the cool concrete and sauntered more than walked over to the trio.

Damn! If he and Jordan don't get back together, I wonder.... Nah, not really my type. But day-um!

"First of all, we watch to see potential clients interact with the dogs. Dogs have amazing instincts, and there are times when we think a person may be a great fit, but the dog won't go near them. Some of these dogs have already been through hell. They aren't fashion accessories or mere pets. They're trained to be on duty for as long as their masters require. We don't get many who pass the testing, but when we do, we want to be sure they will be going to a loving home with a master who will be very consistent with them."

"We've a long way to go to know if the two of you are going to work out as a team. So what he's going to cost you right now is a lot of time because while he's taking care of you, you'll also have to take good care of him."

"I promise I'll do whatever it takes." Gregory bent down in front of River, but the beautiful dog didn't flinch. He reminded Gregory of his encounter with Poochie. He looked up at Larry. "You gave him a command that makes him sit still until you release him, right?"

Larry smiled. "There is that, but basically, if River is on a lead or wearing a service vest, he shouldn't move from his handler's side. I'll give you guys a temp vest and certificate for the ride home, so he won't have to go as cargo."

"You mean I passed? River is coming home with me?"

"Well, to Red Deer and the training center for now," Ron said, "but eventually home with you. If," he said with emphasis, "you two work out."

"We will," Gregory all but shouted. "You bet we will. I can feel it."

For the first time in years, Gregory felt something he thought was lost to him forever.

Hope.

8

Teddy exited the Green Shuttle at the Harmony Transit Center. Ron had offered to meet him at the airport, but Teddy thought that was too much fuss what with parking and all. This was simpler and right now, Teddy needed to keep things as simple as possible. Dale and EJ had insisted Teddy would be more comfortable among friends once her big announcement was made. Teddy could still remember that last argument with EJ.

"There are places that are banning trans men and women from using public bathrooms," EJ argued. "God only knows what other issues may come up."

"What are they going to do, pull down my jeans before I sit on the bowl? If they do, I'm sure I'll pass the panty check. I'm wearing my favorite black lace."

EJ snapped his fingers as he spoke. "I'm sure they're more interested in what's in your black lace."

"EJ, please stop being such a mom. I know you guys have two kids now, but I really don't want to be the third."

EJ hugged Teddy like they would never see each other

again. In a way, they wouldn't because his friend Theodore would not be returning. Ms. Washington would be here forever.

Frankly, Teddy was more concerned about Reuben than the reaction of Paula Blu or general society. He'd not taken it well when Teddy told him their breakup was final, making any number of threats, then showing up at Chances and raising hell. He'd threatened the life of the receptionist, accusing him of wanting Teddy for himself when Edward refused to allow him into the clinic. In the end, the police had to get involved. Teddy had had no choice but to call them and have Reuben arrested. It was that or let her marine clients carry out their threat to stomp the hell out of him. She'd not seen or heard from Reuben since then.

That doesn't mean he's gone or given up.

Teddy's musings were interrupted by the appearance of Ron, Jordan, and a beautiful white shepherd wearing the bright red vest of a service animal.

"Wow, Teddy, you look beautiful! I thought you were just now starting to transition." Ron took one of Teddy's hands and twirled her dance-style. "If I were bi, Jordan and I'd have to talk about including a third."

Jordan stepped up, giving Teddy a tight hug. "He knows better. It's good to see you again." He then indicated the shepherd and said, "This is Deejay. When we're home and he's off duty, he'll get to know you better."

Teddy looked the beautiful white shepherd over with a hesitant glance.

I think I know him as well as I want to.

Ron picked up Teddy's trunk and led the way to Jordan's truck. After they loaded everything in the bed, everyone settled in for the ride to the house.

"I hope you don't mind," Ron said as they pulled out into the road. "I've invited a friend to dinner. He's a huge fan of yours."

"Not at all. I have tickets for you guys for the reunion too. Out of habit, I always plan for a last-minute plus-one. So if your friend wants to come, they're more than welcome."

Just as they pulled up to the house, a taxi was pulling away and Teddy's mouth went dry at the sight of the beautiful man left standing on the side of the driveway.

He punched every one of Teddy's buttons. Tall—at least six feet. Beautiful golden-brown skin. Eyes so dark they almost looked black, and hair styled in soft-looking locks.

Or is that just the way it curls naturally?

She hadn't reacted to a man like this since the day she'd met Reuben. This man was just her type, and right now she wanted to climb up that beautiful body and hang on like a limpet.

"Who is that? Is he single? Please tell me this is your guest and you've invited him to dinner. Hell, *I'll* invite him to dinner."

Jordan laughed. "Down, girl. Yes, that's Gregory. What do you want us to tell him to call you? It seems no one knows your new name, so he only knows you as Phoenix."

"He can call me whatever he wants. After tomorrow night, he'll have better choices."

As Gregory strolled over to the truck, back straight, hips rolling, Teddy took the time to study him from head to foot.

Military man. Probably a marine. I would know that strut if I were blind just from the sound of his heels hitting the ground as he walked.

Teddy released her hair from the ponytail band and met Gregory halfway, hand outstretched.

"You just have to be Ron and Jordan's friend, Gregory. Hi, I'm Teddy, I've heard so much about you." She grinned. "That's a lie. I know very little about you but I'm trusting you to fix that slight deficit."

Gregory's smile outshone the sun. "Well, yes, I'm Gregory, and I'd know that beautiful mane anywhere. You must be Phoenix. I've heard Jordan call you Teddy, but that just doesn't match the beauty standing in front of me." He gently took Teddy's hand. "Welcome to Colorado. What brings you in so early?"

The sound of a throat clearing interrupted the conversation. Ron shoved two suitcases at Gregory, who took them easily. "Here, Starstruck, help with the luggage."

Teddy shouldered her carry-on bag and kissed Gregory on the cheek. "Sexy and strong. My kind of combination. Let's get inside so I can find out what else you got."

The phone was ringing as they walked inside. Ron answered and, after a brief greeting, handed the phone to Teddy. "It's EJ."

"Hey, EJ. I'm just getting in. When do you arrive?"

"That's why I'm calling. I'm so sorry, but we have an emergency with one of our international contracts and I have to leave in the morning for Japan."

Teddy was crestfallen. EJ had planned on going with her to the pre-op appointments at the clinic and being there when she had her first procedure. She'd asked her parents to stay home because she didn't want to be smothered.

Well, time to cowgirl up, I guess.

"It's okay, EJ. I'm good. You go handle your business, I'll handle mine, and maybe you'll be back by the time my procedure's done."

The other end of the line was silent for a moment.

"I'll do my best. Take care, okay? And call me when you finish your appointment this week."

"Are you ever gonna stop being such a mom?"

"Never. I love you, Ms. Phoenix. Good luck with the appointment."

"Okay. Kiss the kids for me. Bye."

Teddy took a long, hard look at the handset before setting it gently in its cradle. She turned around to find Ron, Jordan, and Gregory staring at her, each one looking like he wished someone else would ask if everything was alright.

"Relax, everybody. Nobody died. EJ was supposed to arrive tomorrow to go with me to start my appointments at the Rocky Mountain Surgery Center. He wanted to be there to support me from beginning to end. I knew it would be hard..."

"Wait a minute," Gregory interrupted. "Are you sick? Do you need help? Because I'm on extended leave and am happy to lend a hand. Jordan and I can tell you from experience, scary procedures should not be gone through alone."

"He's right," said Jordan. "Even though I didn't know him, waking up to see Ron at my side was miles better than when I woke up in Walter Reed alone and afraid."

"How about we dial this all back a minute," Ron offered. "Jordan, please show Gregory where to put Teddy's bags while she and I let Deejay out."

With that, Jordan bent over and removed Deejay's harness, then whispered the words, "Salle de Bains." Deejay let out a responding bark and took off like a shot for the doggie door and the freedom of the backyard.

"Is that how you tell him he's off duty?" Gregory asked.

"Nah. Removing the vest means he's off duty. I just told him to go to the bathroom. I use French because I like the way it sounds." Jordan pointed the way down the hall. "Let's go. I think Teddy needs to talk to Ron alone."

Teddy watched the two men move down the hall and then walked to the nearest chair and took a seat.

Ron had gone to the kitchen after the retreating dog and made sure he had water in his dish before returning with a glass of wine. He handed the glass to Teddy and took a seat on the couch.

"Look, you and Gregory just met and there seems to be an instant chemistry between you. I could tell by the way you drank him in when we got here that you're attracted. And believe me, it was quite the sight watching a grown man wiping drool from his chin when he saw you on *Drag Star*." He shifted in his seat, an indication of his discomfort with this conversation. "This is officially none of my business, but I think a trip to the clinic to discuss your top surgery seems like one hell of a first date, especially when the man doesn't even know you're trans."

Teddy let out a wry laugh. She wasn't sure what to do at this point. She only knew canceling this appointment was not an option. "You have to admit, it's one hell of a meet-cute. 'Hello, Gregory, it's great to meet you. I'd love to get to know you better. Oh yeah, did I mention I'm a trans woman? I'm about to have my first procedure. How about we have our first date in the office of the doctor who's going to give me breasts?' Unforgettable."

Teddy shook her head as she rolled the wineglass between his hands. "Can you imagine what he'd say to that?"

"He just might say, 'Hello, Phoenix. It's great to know you too. Not my idea of the ideal first date, but if you throw in lunch after, I'd be glad to be the man that sees you through this.' Actually, no might about it," said Gregory.

Ron and Teddy turned toward the living room door to see him standing at the threshold.

"I came to get your last bag," he said as he picked up the duffle. "Look, me offering this may seem fast, but I've learned that the only thing to do in the suck is gather whatever resources you can and push through." He dropped the bag and walked over to Teddy, then stooped down in front of her. "I don't bite, I promise. Well, that is, unless you want me to."

He then stood, retrieved the dropped duffle, and headed down the hall.

Teddy watched Gregory move back down the hall.

Now that's one fine ass.

"The pleasure will be all mine, Mario."

DINNER WAS a bit more somber than the light evening among friends originally planned. Gregory had meant his offer to accompany Teddy to the clinic appointment, and he needed to make that clear.

Breasts, huh. Well, she's a damn fine woman.

"Teddy, I'm one hundred percent in none-of-my-business territory here, but, guessing from the conversation I overheard, you're a trans woman and your appointments are at the Rocky Mountain Surgery Center in the foothills." Gregory took a deep drink from his wineglass before continuing. "I just want you to know I meant what I said about going with you to your appointments, and I still mean it. Support's important."

As Gregory finished, Jordan spoke up. "I'll drive! EJ isn't the only family you have. You've got me and Ron and Deejay."

Deejay had been lying on his blanket but barked and ran into the dining room in response to hearing his name.

Everybody laughed as Jordan said, "See, it's unanimous."

That broke the tension that had been circulating the room from the moment EJ called and Gregory overheard Ron and Teddy's conversation.

"There you go," Gregory added. "Not only will our first date be unusual, but apparently, we'll also be chaperoned."

9

As it turned out, Jordan drove only Teddy to the clinic for her pre-operative evaluation. Ron and Gregory had to keep a training appointment with River, and Teddy wasn't sure how she felt about having a relative stranger with her for such an important visit.

Her reaction to meeting Gregory had caused her to consider the possibility of feelings she thought long dead. She needed to discuss the possibilities with Dr. Branson and Janice.

"Miss Washington!" announced the nurse and Teddy rose to follow her.

"Damn, they're real formal here," Jordan commented. "Deejay and I will be waiting for you here."

"Relax, Jordan. They don't deadname as a matter of practice. My last name will remain Washington, but I can't give them a new first name until after the reunion." Teddy shrugged her shoulders. "My mom gave me my new name and it's in an envelope back at the house. I'll learn what it is at the same time as the rest of the world, when I read her message on stage."

"Look, I don't even pretend to know all I probably should about transitioning, but it seems to me too much of this is tied to your drag life." Jordan stood and hugged Teddy. "I'm just saying, this is your real life and it's going to be hard enough. You may be a public figure, but the most important decisions you'll ever make, until you marry, shouldn't be fodder for the public eye." He'd released Deejay's leash and now reached down to reattach it. "Go on, talk to your doctor, girl. He's the expert. Me, I'm just a fucked-up vet trying to be a friend to someone who was there for me when I needed it the most. What the hell do I know?" He signaled Deejay and headed for a door that opened to an atrium. "I'll be out there when you're ready."

Teddy moved on into the examination room where Dr. Branson was waiting along with her counselor, Janice Taylor.

Dr. Branson spoke first. "If it's alright with you, I'd like to address you as Teddy since we have no other options and Miss Washington sounds so formal for our relationship." He looked toward the door. "Where is your friend?" He referred to his clipboard. "EJ? I thought he was going to be your support partner for this part of your journey."

Agreeing to the doctor's use of her deadname for this short time, Teddy sat on the exam table. "EJ had a work emergency. The friend I'm staying with is here waiting in the atrium. He and his husband aannd"—she drug out the "and" for emphasis—"someone new in my life. Gregory."

"Someone new?" asked Janice. "Have you resolved things with Reuben? I mean, even if you did, you're making a lot of life-altering decisions all at the same time." She paused for effect and then said softly, "Teddy, you haven't figured out what to call yourself, have you?" She stood and led Teddy from the exam table to a third chair that had been placed in the room. "Most of our patients begin using a new name at the beginning of their transition. You're about to have your first surgery in a few weeks, and we still don't know what you want to be called." She took Teddy's hands in hers. "I guess what I'm asking is, are you sure you're ready for this right now?"

"Surgery is an option always open to you here," Dr. Branson interjected. "We're not trying to stop you. We just want to prevent, if possible, the meltdown that can be caused by milestone overload."

"I know I'm confusing everyone, so let me start with the name situation. My mom is my biggest cheerleader. She is also where I get my dramatic flair."

"Hence the hair?" asked Janice. "I'm loving the new color, by the way."

"The hair started a long time ago. I guess mothers always know." Teddy shifted in her seat. "Here's the thing. When I announced my decision to begin surgical transition, she only asked one thing of me. You see, she named me Theodora before I was born. When I was assigned male at birth, she changed it to Theodore. She asked to be able to name me for my rebirth. She and I agree Theodora doesn't fit. It's a request made of love and support, and I won't deny her that. My official birthday will be that Friday, and that's when we'll all know my new name."

This time it was Dr. Branson with questions. "So, who's this Gregory?"

"I just met him and yes, we do seem to have an amazing first-meet chemistry. I mean, I want things I didn't care about before. So, I've got serious questions. For instance, if it's just the hormone replacement therapy like people say, why didn't I feel this way around Reuben?"

Dr. Branson smiled. "Teddy, many people, including

trans women, say sexual arousal is connected to their attraction and emotional response to their partner."

Janice added, "There have been some small-scale studies, but as you can probably understand, it's not a topic a lot of people, male or female, are willing to be candid about. So, more on Gregory?"

"He was there when EJ called and had to cancel. Gregory stepped up, but even I thought that was a bit much so soon, especially since I always had Ron and Jordan as plan B."

"You didn't say you had a plan B," said Dr. Branson. "That alone makes me feel better about your approach to the surgery. I'm guessing Gregory knows you're transitioning, so if this relationship continues, remember what we said about communication." He clapped both hands together. "Okay, let's get to the medical stuff. This is a pre-op visit, after all."

Janice rose and walked to the door. "That's my cue." She laid a card on the counter. "If you're comfortable with it, bring Gregory with you to our session Wednesday." She gave Teddy a hug and slipped out the door.

10

The drive back into Red Deer felt tense and Teddy couldn't figure what could possibly be wrong with Jordan.

Well, communication is key!

"Jordan, is something wrong? There's a strange vibe in the air that wasn't around when we left out this morning."

"I need to apologize. What I said about how you handle your life was out of line. I'm so used to the guys in group, I guess I just wasn't thinking."

"Jordan, I lead groups like yours. If I had a thin skin, I couldn't do my job. Besides, only a friend would step in like you did, so we're good." Teddy looked out the window and realized they were not heading back the way they came. "Are we going somewhere?"

"Uh, yeah. We're meeting Ron and Gregory at Vincent's for drinks and dinner because there's somebody Gregory wants you to meet." Jordan was grinning as he spoke.

"Speaking of Gregory, the last I'd heard he was a tree-sized thorn in your side. Now you guys are all but braiding each other's hair. When did the two of you become BFFs?"

"We're okay. We all have our stuff. I got huffy because one day in group, Gregory called me on mine." Jordan gave a short laugh. "The thing was, he was right that day and it hit home. I was whining, despite all I had, and here was Gregory struggling to just exist. He made me see how comparatively small my problems were."

"That's the blessing and curse of therapy. Vets are one group of brothers and sisters that will call you on your shit."

"You got that right!" Jordan laughed, Teddy joined in, and Deejay barked in agreement. That's how Ron found them when the truck parked in Vincent's lot, the cacophony of laughing and barking announcing their arrival.

"What in the hell is going on in here?"

Teddy had tears rolling down her eyes. "It's one of those things that would lose meaning in the retelling."

"Yeah, Ron," Jordan added. "You just had to be there."

Teddy hopped out of the truck, then opened the back door to let Deejay out. Instead, the dog remained rooted to his seat behind Jordan. "Well, damn. Was it something I said?"

"Nah," Ron responded. "That's his training. He won't leave the truck until Jordan does. Funny thing is, he's only supposed to be that way when he's on duty, but they are so bonded it no longer matters. He sticks to Jordan like a second skin."

"I bet that makes bedtime interesting."

"You have no idea, but I think you may soon find out." Ron pointed to Vincent's patio entrance. "Gregory's waiting for you."

"Are you and Jordan coming?"

"No. We've got other plans."

Teddy looked up to see Gregory standing near the patio entrance. Next to him stood a beautiful Portuguese water dog. Teddy approached and bent down as if to pet the pup, but the dog took one step back, just out of reach.

"This is River," said a smiling Gregory. "He won't let you pet him when he's working. No offense, but unless and until we know each other better, I'd prefer it that way."

"None taken," Teddy said as she stood up and stepped away from the pup.

"Woah, wait. You can pet me all you want." Gregory stepped forward and planted a light kiss on Teddy's lips. "Was everything okay at your appointment?"

"Yeah, I'm good to go Monday after the reunion." Teddy looked around the patio. "Nice place, but Jordan said you promised me dinner. I'm presuming River is part of the chaperone team?"

"Yeah. He goes wherever I go and, if it all works out, that includes back to work. In the meantime, our table is waiting. Shall we?" Gregory offered his arm to Teddy and led her towards the dining room where a table for two had been set up with cutlery, wineglasses, a small candle in a glass, and an envelope centered in front of the seat he guided Teddy to.

Teddy opened the envelope. "What's this?" she said as she extracted the card inside.

You started in my dreams as Phoenix, an imaginary queen.

Now you're here, real and hopefully in my life.

I don't know where this road we're on is leading.

I'm just happy to be walking it with you.

"That's beautiful. Thank you." Teddy carefully returned the card to its envelope. "I wasn't sure if you felt the same strange connection I did and I didn't know how to approach it." She fiddled with the envelope as she spoke. "I have so much going on: the reunion, my hopefully not-short tenure as reigning queen, my surgery, and last of all, an ex-boyfriend who may be less than accepting of his new place out of my life." She raised her eyes to look at Gregory.

Damn, fate is cruel to bring you into my life at this time.

Gregory smiled. The candlelight radiating on his face made him appear almost ethereal. "I'm not asking you to marry me. I'm not even trying to get you to move in. I have some pretty intense issues going on myself. I've taken every bad and crazy thing life has thrown at me and not necessarily in stride. So, I'll be damned if I'm going to pass up the opportunity to embrace the possibility of something good." He reached out and took Teddy's hands, carefully placing the envelope back on the table. "Meeting you can't be an accident. I believe there's a good purpose behind it for me. I guess I'm saying I hope it's a good thing for you too."

"We'll see," said Teddy. "But not unless you feed me first. I'm starved."

11

The Hughes Stadium, once proud home to the Colorado State University Aggies, sits east of the Horsetooth Reservoir in the shadow of the huge rock emblazoned with a giant "A". Though the Aggies have moved on to their new home at the fully modern on-campus stadium in central Red Deer, the students still faithfully sojourn every year to refresh the glowing white paint and celebrate the upcoming season.

The stadium, still owned by the state, is leased as a venue for concerts, tent revivals and right now, for the viewing of the finale and live reunion of the contestants. This oft-forgotten space was going down in history as the site where Phoenix, the reigning *Drag Star* Queen, rocked the stage and sent shock waves through the drag world for all eternity.

Ask any New York resident where they were during the great blackout of 2003, they can tell you. Everyone can tell you, like it was yesterday, where they were when Hurricane Katrina caused the Mississippi River to rise and break through the levies. Now, and for the foreseeable future, anyone who pays the slightest attention to the world of drag entertainment will be able to relay their exact location the night Phoenix rose from the ashes and set the drag world ablaze.

The three weeks leading up to this night had been a balm for Teddy's soul. Gregory had been true to his word and accompanied Teddy to the remainder of her appointments. He carried a small notebook with him and took notes as Teddy and the counselor spoke of the possible continued effects of HRT and the changes in Teddy's sexual responses and what they entailed.

After each appointment, they'd do some fun thing together, like the times they wandered through Lucille's Closet, a boutique attached to the surgery center, and Gregory helped Teddy pick out what they'd begun to call her interim wardrobe, stylishly cute and appropriately comfortable for the post-op period.

One more memorable time was the day Gregory surprised her with an excursion into the foothills along the highway 287 corridor.

"This isn't the way back to Ron's." They'd borrowed Jordan's truck that day and Teddy was sure they promised to return in time for Jordan to leave for classes. Gregory had detoured off the main road onto highway 287. She'd only been in this part of Red Deer a short time, but Teddy had begun to memorize landmark points in the trip between Ron's ranch, the surgery center, and downtown Red Deer.

"I know. We're going sightseeing. I've got something cool to show you." He'd raised his eyebrows and smiled as he interrupted Teddy's next sentence. "I cleared it with Jordan. Ron is going to drop him off at school. I'll pick him up after my training session with River."

In no time at all, Gregory had pulled up in front of an

obviously closed building. The weatherworn paint had seen better days and it was clearly shuttered down.

Teddy hopped out and noted the sign resembling a hollowed-out snare drum. "Virginia Dale Café, " she read aloud as she approached and noted a crude painted sign across the door. "U.S. Post Office? Now here's a full-service operation. Where are we, Hooterville?"

Teddy couldn't stop laughing as she stepped up to the hitching post in front of the café slash post office and posed for the pictures Gregory began taking with his phone.

"Welcome to Virginia Dale, Colorado," he said as he grabbed her hand and took off running down the roadside.

"Where are we going now?" Teddy asked as she thought, *Oh my god. He's too cute, and I can't believe we're running around the foothills like lunatics.*

"Church," Gregory said, laughing, as they stopped in front of a small, white, chapel-like building complete with a steeple housing a bell tower.

"This thing is like something out of the Waltons, or one of those old west shows." Teddy cocked her head and took in the rest of the view. These were the only buildings and unlike the café, the church seemed to be in current use. A sign hung from a t-post announced, "The Reverend Peter Goode as pastor of the Virginia Dale Church with services every Sunday at eleven o'clock." The mountains were snow-capped, and the air was so clean it almost tasted sweet. She thought, *I could almost see myself living here. Well, as long as I could get to the shops and reality.*

"We got here in no time, yet we're in the middle of nowhere. Seriously, where are we?"

Gregory walked up behind Teddy, wrapped his arms around her waist, and placed a light kiss on the back of her neck. He pointed to what looked like a small cluster of buildings off in the distance. "We're in the unincorporated community of Virginia Dale. Those buildings down there make up the heart of the place. It doesn't look like it, but it's a tourist attraction, complete with hotels and tour guides."

"Oh yeah? So, does this tour have a chuck wagon, cuz this girl is hungry," Teddy said as she turned in Gregory's arms. "You kidnapped me. You plan on feeding me?" She had then reached up, placed her arms around his neck, and kissed Gregory, who moved one hand to the back of her neck as the kiss deepened to one fed by an unexpected passion. Just as Teddy began to think, *Hmmm, maybe eating is overrated*, Gregory pulled back from the kiss.

"I'd take you down the road to the Wagon Wheel. It's a great place, but we need to get back. River's training is my ticket to real freedom and we're about to graduate soon."

The memory of that kiss was so intense, Teddy shivered as she relived the moment. They fit together so well. Most of all, she'd found in Gregory a kindred spirit.

They'd each talked about the path life had put them on. She smiled when she remembered Gregory calling her a drag queen counselor. It brought her fondly back to the day when EJ had coined the same phrase on learning what his friend had been doing in her off-duty hours. Back then, EJ had been going through a hard time. *Maybe the universe is trying to give me some of mine back,* she thought as she considered how Gregory appeared in her life at a time when she needed someone the most.

A major highlight of their burgeoning relationship had been Teddy's developing relationship with River. She was surprised to learn her first meeting at Vincent's was also a training run. River had passed with flying colors.

Ron had adjusted Gregory's training schedule around Teddy's appointments at the clinic, and Teddy was able to watch as Gregory and River went through their training in the various movie-set scenarios created to teach the service dogs agility and behavior in crowds, stores, and parks, and around children and curious adults. The volunteer actors enjoyed the role play, but each man, woman, and child took their job seriously.

The training was going well, and River was with Gregory all the time now. For her part, Teddy had learned what to do to help if he had a seizure and how to distinguish between seizures and panic attacks since Gregory's physical responses appeared to be the same.

One afternoon, Gregory had wanted to show Teddy around Loveland, the iconic mountain town situated between Denver and Red Deer.

"When I'm able to afford my own home, this is where I want to live," he'd said as they drove down the main street. "It's close enough to Denver and Red Deer to have easy access to either city." He turned into a parking lot and stopped, pointing in front of them. The view took Teddy's breath away. The snowcapped mountains were majestic.

Gregory pulled into an open space in front of Café Braggi. The hostess met them at the door and led them to a table situated by the huge windows, affording them a continued view of the mountains. The food had been superior, and Teddy couldn't help but think, *Now this is the way to spend an afternoon.*

That day had ended as most did for them, at Gregory's apartment, but that night was different. That time, Teddy stayed, and they'd made love for the first time that night.

Gregory had been patient, careful to move at Teddy's pace, and ever mindful of what made Teddy feel good. It had been both tender and intense, and Teddy felt like she was flying, weightless through the air as she called out Gregory's name over and over again.

Even now, as Teddy remembered that night, the amazing sensation wrapped around her. So much so, she barely heard the stagehand signal it was time for Phoenix to make her appearance.

Adjusting the crown, Teddy walked slowly to the platform the way they'd rehearsed, timing her steps to the soft music that announced the queen's arrival.

This is it. Goodbye, Theodore!

Clutching in a gloved hand the envelope given to her by her mother, Teddy quickly sat in the carriage which would dramatically lower Phoenix to the stage.

To her surprise, Phoenix's confessional played loud and clear as the carriage descended smoothly on the supporting ropes. Behind Phoenix stood a scantily clad Adonis who kept whispering in her ear, "You're only human, you're only human."

Phoenix was so nervous, the dramatic reenactment of the return of victors to Rome was almost lost on her as she realized this was not exactly what had been rehearsed.

Okay, Paula, I guess it's game time.

Paula stood downstage as the young man led Phoenix by the hand and presented her with great flourish to her public. Paula gave an exaggerated curtsey as the season's contestants artfully arranged on either side either cheered and tossed rose petals to drop at her feet or scowled as they let the petals fall where they stood.

Fortunately, there were so few of the latter that no one in the auditorium noticed. They were too stunned by the words of the confessional. The audience was hard to see, but Phoenix could clearly hear the cheers and exclamations of shock.

Paula wore an unreadable expression as she took her seat next to Phoenix.

"Phoenix, dahling, were your ears ringing? We have been discussing your exciting competition performances on and off set all night long. It seems your entrance has cleared up some of the rumors. So, tell us, dahling, how did you come to this grand decision and why announce it here?"

Slowly, Phoenix began to relay the edited story of feeling like her skin no longer fit. She skated past Paula's damning statement and instead phrased it as the "current climate of the day."

Dabbing tears from her eyes, she said, "I have always wanted to be just who I am. I hate fake people and here I was, lying to myself and my sisters. I couldn't stand it anymore."

Suddenly, a flurry of feathers and rhinestones in five-inch heels swarmed around Phoenix. In the middle of the swarm, dressed in her signature, ice-white gown, stood Alaska.

"Phoenix, my sister, my forever queen. We love you and want you to know we wish you the best in your journey to not only find your truth but also in your desire to make our world a safe place for trans men and women everywhere."

She pushed through the standing contestants as they began to applaud and addressed the audience. "Don't just sit there slack-jawed! If you agree with Phoenix, get off your ass and onto your feet and let her know that she's right, that the time has come for all of us to move forward and make the world safe for everyone to be who you are!"

The crowd roared as they all came to their feet clapping and stomping. Not everyone was happy, however, and as the fervor died down and the contestants returned to their seats, one lone figure stood center stage...Peaches.

Paula smiled. "Peaches? Do you have something you want to say?" Phoenix thought the smile she wore looked more like the smirk of a serpent about to pounce.

What the hell is she up to?

As Peaches strode forward, Phoenix couldn't help but think the dress, seemingly designed to resemble a peach, looked more like a big orange crepe paper ball, not unlike the ones you buy at the party store and open into shape with little metal fold-over clips holding the ends together.

If she comes for me on this stage, I'm gonna bare her ugly ass on nationwide television.

"I'm confused, Phoenix. Are you a man or a woman? Seems to me you're just whatever suits your purpose at the time."

Alaska stood. "Yes, Peaches, honey, you look confused. I guess that explains the dime-store costume you're wearing tonight."

Peaches face turned beet red. She stood facing Alaska, both hands curled into fists. "So, are you the mother of this freak of nature or its lawyer?"

Alaska let out a hearty laugh. "You better relax your hands and sit the fuck down, girl. I promise, you don't even wanna mess with Phoenix's mother. I hear she'll cut a bitch over her baby girl."

Phoenix was about to get up when she saw Paula signal security to approach the stage. She was losing control of this shit show. "Go to commercial," she screamed as she stepped between the two screaming queens. "Girls! Girls! This is not what this reunion is supposed to be about. Alaska, sit your ass down. Peaches, don't forget our little talk before the finale. This is not a daytime talk show. We are not going to be rolling in the aisles."

The audience, of course, was eating all of this up. Shouts of *fight, fight, fight* rang out all over the place.

Her speech helped Paula get order restored, and she signaled a man in the wings who quietly led Peaches off the stage.

There goes one unhappy bitch.

Phoenix returned her attention to Paula, who was once again reading from her cue cards.

"So, Phoenix, I guess you did set it off, after all." She looked at the audience with a smirk. "Well, it can't be a family reunion without an emergency or somebody going to jail, right?" The audience laughed knowingly. "Have you decided on your new birth name?"

Damn, she really is good at this. Well, so am I.

"Actually, Paula, we're all going to learn my new birth name at the same time."

Paula looked perplexed. "Are you trying to tell me you don't know what your name is? How is that possible?"

"When I was born, my mother whispered my name in my ear and then announced it to the world. She's not doing that now because we didn't know what the setup here would be, but she sealed it in this envelope instead."

"Before we go further, Phoenix, I know your mom is here, and as a surprise, we brought your parents backstage once you stepped on the stage." She signaled the stage manager and announced, "Ladies and gentlemen, please welcome Nathan and Laura Washington!"

Laura strolled out holding the world's most beautiful bouquet. It looked like she was holding flame. She walked over to Phoenix, placed the bouquet in her lap, kissed her on the cheek, and whispered in her ear. Nathan followed suit and then the couple took seats on the couch placed near Phoenix.

Paula addressed Laura. "If I have this right, I understand you have an announcement you want to make."

"That's right, Paula." Laura stood, grabbed Phoenix's hand, and led her to the center of the stage. Tears flowed as the two women held hands. There was not a dry eye anywhere. Phoenix looked over toward Paula as an *awwww* resounded from the audience followed by thunderous applause.

Damn! Even Paula is crying.

When the applause died down and everyone took their seats, Nathan joined them to stand on Phoenix's other side and Paula handed Laura the microphone.

Laura's voice rang out clear and strong as she announced, "Ladies and gentlemen, I present to you, my daughter, Phoenix, the reigning queen of *Drag Star*, now and forever also known as Ms. Destiny Washington!"

12

The victory celebrations lasted well into the evening. Destiny's parents said their goodbyes and retired to their hotel early as they had a plane to catch in the morning. Laura hugged Destiny and Gregory repeatedly, insisting they call her immediately after Destiny's surgery to let her know the outcome.

"Are you sure you don't want me to stay? Who's going to take care of you after your surgery?"

"I'm a grown woman, Mom, and I've got this. Besides, Gregory will have my back, not to mention Ron and Jordan. If all else fails, I've got Deejay and River."

"Deejay, I can see, but River will just cute you to death." She bent over to pet the curly-haired dog and Gregory stepped back, taking River with him.

"I'm sorry, Ms. Laura. Remember, no one is allowed to pet River, especially when he's working."

Laura smiled. "I'm sorry, I forgot. He is a beautiful dog." She turned to Destiny. "Now him, I like. Reuben is going to be green with envy."

Destiny tried to remain calm at the mention of her ex.

She'd told no one of the multiple calls and texts from Reuben that she'd received. At first, they were the usual apologies, promises to change, and pleas to take him back. Lately though, there'd been threats.

She bid her parents goodbye and waved after their departing car just as her phone rang again. She answered, intending to ask Reuben for the last time to leave her alone, but was stunned into silence as Reuben interrupted her. His speech was growly and slurred as he graphically described the ways in which he intended to give her the gender-affirming surgery she so "desperately craved."

Destiny pressed end but it wasn't over. A text message came through from an unknown number and contained graphic imagery described as the "new and improved Theodora Washington."

That one shook Destiny to her core, and while the humans may not have noticed, Deejay and River both alerted their masters. Jordan was the first to respond. "I'm okay, boy. S'asseoir." Deejay complied, immediately sitting quietly on his haunches at Jordan's side. River, on the other hand, was not so easily convinced. Gregory looked to Ron for guidance.

"Relax, Gregory, You and River are still new to this. Are you feeling alright?"

"I'm fine, but we probably all need to turn in for the night."

Ron nodded in agreement. "Why don't we all go back to the ranch? It's closer and Destiny still needs to retrieve her stuff from the dressing room tomorrow."

"Good point." Gregory agreed as he moved to place an arm around Destiny.

"Babe, you're shaking! What's the matter?" He pulled off his jacket and placed it around Destiny's shoulders, then leaned in to kiss her but stopped. "Okay, Destiny, what's wrong? Talk to me."

Destiny could barely speak. She knew Reuben could be harmful when he was angry, but this was a whole new level of crazy. She couldn't find the words she needed, so she handed her phone to Gregory, who then passed it to Ron.

"Let's get to the truck," was Ron's only response.

The ride to Ron's ranch was silent. The jubilation of the evening had been dampened by the threatening text from Reuben. Once inside, Gregory and Jordan released River and Deejay to the backyard. The two dogs had begun to bond and raced through the doggie door to romp freely until their masters summoned them.

Ron offered everyone their choice of wine, beer, soda, or water, and once everybody was settled in the family room chairs, drinks in hand, Ron began to speak.

"Destiny, this is over the top. We should notify the police."

"Unless he's here in Red Deer, what are the police going to be able to do?" asked Jordan.

"I have to admit, the threat disturbed the hell out of me, but now that I've calmed down, I still don't believe Reuben would leave his job, where he is so very valuable, and come to Colorado for the sole purpose of hunting me down. He doesn't know where I'm staying. He doesn't know anything about Gregory, and he never watches *Drag Star*."

"Are you sure?" Gregory interjected. "Maybe the show tonight set him off."

Destiny took a deep breath. She believed deep in her soul that Reuben was truly trying to scare her into coming back home and forgetting about the gender-affirming surgery. *He can and has been physical, but not like that.* "He's blowing off steam. This is the first time I've left him and stuck to it. Besides, he called me Theodora, not Destiny. If he'd watched the show, he would have called me Destiny."

"Well, if it's okay with you," said Ron. "I'm going to call New York in the morning and have EJ or Dale make sure Reuben is still in town. That boy sounds crazy. My motto is, when people show you who they are, believe them."

"That's fair. In the meantime, I'm exhausted and need to go to bed."

"Sure, you do," laughed Jordan. "Just keep it down."

Gregory whistled for River and took Destiny's hand to lead her down the hall. "You two just be mindful to take your own advice."

∽

Ron watched Destiny and Gregory walk down the hall. "I'm concerned about this situation."

Jordan agreed. "Me too. During my short stay in Sayville, Reuben showed up at Chances. When he left, he had Ted—I mean, Destiny in tow. She returned and handled group, but we all knew something was wrong. I don't know the outcome, but I do know Dale was pissed off, and Reuben never showed up at Chances again."

Jordan sat on the couch and Deejay moved to place his head on Jordan's lap.

Ron noticed the move and became concerned. "Did that bastard do or say something to you?"

"If he had, I'd have kicked his ass. I've got serious skills even with one leg. I'm worried about Destiny though. If Reuben is smart, he won't approach her while she's with Gregory. That would be his last mistake in life." He shook his head as he stroked Deejay's soft down. "The thing is, Gregory is going back to work soon, and he has a board appearance coming up. He can't be with Destiny all the time."

"Isn't her surgery scheduled for Monday?" Ron picked up the phone. "Never mind, I'm calling Sayville to find out if EJ and Dale are able to confirm Reuben is still there. If not, we're calling police. This is getting out of hand."

Deejay let out a bark as if to say, "Damn right."

13

When Gregory awoke, holding Destiny's body in his arms felt like he'd finally come home.

Damn, I'm a lucky man. Who knew one night could be so perfect?

He reached down and softly stroked the thigh that lay across his hips. The rest of Destiny's body lined up alongside his in a perfect fit. Gregory chuckled to himself as he recalled teasing friends who talked about how well a partner fit next to them.

What do you know? It really is a thing.

Destiny's hair fell softly over her face and brushed Gregory's chest like a whisper. He inhaled deeply, loving the scent of the product she used. Destiny had been shaken and had clung to Gregory. In spite of the events of the evening, holding her close made every single fiber of his body feel amazing. Lovemaking had been infrequent for them as they navigated the waters of Destiny's new normal. Still, he'd never felt so satisfied in a relationship.

However, his mind was troubled, and he wasn't sure where to begin to find a resolution. *There is a woman inside the man underneath the drag. I always thought Phoenix was awesome. I was attracted to Teddy on sight and wanted more than anything to get to know her. Having Destiny in my arms makes me feel like I hit the lottery. So, what does that make me? Is there a name for me? Hell, why do I have to label myself at all to be Destiny's person?*

In the days leading up to the reunion show, he'd come to care for the redheaded firebrand. They'd discussed the unbelievable speed of their storybook-like romance, but they surged forward all the same.

Their whirlwind relationship had been such that Destiny's surgeon had asked to meet and speak to Gregory and Destiny together. Gregory didn't resist. He couldn't imagine what they could possibly need from him, but he'd come to a point where he was willing to do anything to make this journey go smoothly for Destiny.

Now I understand why Dr. Branson gave me his card. He knew this day would come.

Gregory closed his eyes and could still hear Dr. Branson instruct Destiny.

"You need to consider all the relationships in your life. Once you affirm your gender, you may find you have to leave some people behind." The young doctor looked at Destiny. "This is not just about changing your name and augmenting your breasts. This is the beginning of you living the rest of your life as who you were meant to be, without compromise or apologies."

He then turned to Gregory. "I know this relationship is a new one, and I usually advise against it, but you two seem to have become uniquely well-suited over these last three weeks. Being in her life is serious business. Questions you never considered may cross your mind or rudely come from others." He'd handed Gregory a business card.

"When those questions come, don't go to Google. Call me."

Looks like I may be making that call today. I want to be everything Destiny needs me to be, and to do that, I've got to make sure of who I am so she can be sure.

He leaned over and kissed the top of the sleep-tussled head as Destiny began to stir. "Good morning, beautiful."

Destiny stretched like a cat and then curled back around Gregory, indicating she had no intention of rising yet.

Gregory heard a whimper and turned his head to see two large brown eyes staring at him with expectation. *Damn!* He gently lifted Destiny's face to meet his and kissed her. "I love morning cuddles, but I need to let River out first."

"I'll be right here when you get back." Destiny did a catlike stretch and as Gregory got out of the bed, he could have sworn he heard a sound much like a purr. *Damn, that's hot. I bet she's a Leo. Bring the fire, baby!! It's about time the stars aligned in my favor. Yeah, it's a good day to be a Sagittarius.*

Gregory whistled as he walked into the kitchen, more drawn by the enticing aroma of fresh coffee than the need to tend to River's morning routine.

"Welcome to service dog ownership." Ron laughed as Gregory directed River to the dog door leading to the backyard. "Morning lie-ins are not in the cards. If you intend to build a relationship that includes romantic nights and morning cuddles, you better build a routine for River that keeps that time in mind."

"Yeah, I gotta do that," Gregory said. "Did you talk to the folks in Sayville?" He walked over to the counter and took down a cup.

"I did. Seems Reuben was spotted in town yesterday, so you better pull down another cup. You both have a busy day ahead of you."

While Gregory set to making two cups of coffee, Ron continued passing along information.

"So, that Paula person from the show called." Ron said Paula's name like he'd just bitten into something sour, clearly showing his disdain. "The stadium is requesting every prop and costume be picked up right away as they need the space for a concert scheduled for tomorrow."

Gregory laughed at Ron's theatrics. "Calm down, Ron. We're planning to go collect her stuff after I get back from River's run-through at the store."

"I'm afraid that won't do. Ms. *Pawwwla* has made it perfectly clear that this must be accomplished this *mawning* as the stadium organizers are throwing an absolute *hissy*!" Ron waltzed around the room using a tea towel as a hanky and flinging it to and fro as he gave extra enunciation to *Paula*, *morning*, and *absolute hissy*.

Gregory laughed so hard he spilled the coffee in his cup, slipped on the liquid, and fell to the floor, causing a barking River to run over and examine his master. Deejay, unimpressed, moved to his bowl and began eating his morning kibble. The commotion apparently awakened Jordan and finally roused Destiny, as the two appeared in the kitchen simultaneously.

Destiny was first to speak. She kneeled next to Gregory, who was rolled into a ball and clutching his stomach as he tried to calm the coughing fit that accompanied his laughing. "Are you alright? What in the hell is going on in here?"

Gregory rose to his knees and quieted the barking and pacing River. He then took Destiny's hands and the two stood. "I'm fine. Ron was doing an amazing imitation of Paula Blu as he was repeating the message she left for you."

He reached over to the counter and handed Destiny a cup of coffee. "She wants you gals to pick up your stuff today, which is a problem because River and I are due at the store in an hour."

"So we'll just go this evening, like we planned."

"No," Ron said. "They need everybody's stuff out this afternoon at the latest. Apparently, most of the girls took their stuff last night. It seems only you and Alaska are left."

"Okay, so I'll call an Uber to take me there. I've been hauling my trunks and suitcases for years. I got this."

"But," interrupted Gregory, "what about Reuben?" He didn't want to express his fear that Reuben could easily have made his way to Colorado between the time he was last seen in Sayville and now. In fact, MacArthur Airport was only a ten-minute drive from even the furthest point in the little hamlet. He remembered thinking he and Ron could have easily walked to the training center when they went to retrieve River in Patchogue.

"Listen, gang. You guys are going to work and train River. Jordan is going to do whatever Jordan does, and I am going to get my drag from the stadium and pack for my surgery admission."

As if on cue, Jordan filled a travel cup with coffee and, after giving Ron a kiss, bid everyone goodbye. As he and Deejay walked out the front door, Gregory realized he had no idea what Jordan did with his time all day. "Where's Jordan going so early?"

"He takes weekend classes at the university," Ron answered before gulping the rest of his coffee in one drink. "Speaking of which, you need to get showered and dressed cuz we're gonna be late if you don't." He then turned to Destiny. "Feel free to make yourself whatever you want for breakfast. You've been here before, so you know your way around the house. The spare key is on the hook by the door."

Well, I guess that settles it.

Unfortunately, Gregory didn't feel settled. In fact, he couldn't shake the feeling of doom that had become a warning beacon for him ever since the morning he and his men left for the scouting trip that damn near took his life. The only thing he could do was what he'd always done–pray.

Lord, I'm putting Destiny in your hands. Please protect her as only you can.

Gregory showered, dressed, and packed the go bag he'd learned to carry with him since he and Destiny had become close. He never knew where the night was going to end, so having extra clean clothes and a supply of his meds made life happen without being awkward. *A marine is always prepared for anything. Ooorah!*

He joined Ron in the kitchen to find River already in his vest and ready for work. After kissing Destiny, he said to Ron, "Let's do it! I'm ready." As they walked to the car, he turned to see Destiny waving goodbye from the door. Just then, a chill ran through him, and he shivered.

"It is a cool morning," said Ron. "Want to stop by yours and pick up a different jacket?"

"Nah, it's not cold. It's what happens when I get a premonition." Gregory hated when he got those, and he always regretted it when he ignored them. The chill always made him feel like what his mother described as a ghost crossing your grave.

He climbed into the truck after letting River in. "I don't trust this Reuben character. I'd like to go straight to the coliseum once we're done to make sure Destiny has gotten her stuff without incident."

14

Just as Destiny stepped from the shower, her phone rang. She looked at the caller ID.

Lord, please don't let this be Reuben. I am not in the mood for his crazy ass.

Fortunately, it was Alaska. "Hey, bitch. What are you up to?"

"Calling your lazy ass. It seems we are the last of the Mohicans and need to go pack our drag and evacuate the premises."

"Yeah, I was just putting myself together so I can call an Uber and get down there and back before Gregory returns."

A scream rent the air through the phone. "Girrrrl, you slut!! You done let that man tap that ass? I'm so jealous. How is it I've been living in Colorado all my life and never ran into that tall, dark hunk of lusciousness?"

"Simmer, girl, cuz he's off the market as long as I have anything to say about it." Destiny cast a quick look at her watch. *Damn it's getting late!* "Listen, I gotta get moving so I can be there before noon like they asked."

"That's why I was calling. I can scoop you up and we can

do lunch after we grab our drag. There's this place in town called Vincent's. He and his husband cook their asses off and they're big *Drag Star* fans."

"Alright, I'm a recent patron of their amazing skills, so you've sold me. Now, get the hell off the phone and let me get ready."

By the time Destiny had showered and dressed, Alaska was vigorously knocking on the door.

"Damn, girl, you trying to blow the door down?"

"No, but I did want your deaf ass to hear me," said Alaska, whose non-drag name was Anthony Garvin. Dressed in jeans, a sweatshirt, and basketball sneakers, Anthony walked in like he owned the place. He took Destiny's hand and twirled her as if dancing. "Damn! When's the surgery because those hormones are definitely doing their job." He dropped her hand and stepped back, whistling. "Ooh wee, just stay away from my man so I don't have to kill you both. So when do we start calling you Destiny for real? Cuz damn if you look anything like the Theodore I once knew."

"Actually, the center has a legal staff handling all my name-change paperwork. They're walking my job through the HR stuff because New York isn't quite ready yet, you know."

"Girl, why do you think I live in Colorado in the first place? It damn sure ain't for the weather."

Together, they left the house and headed for Anthony's Jetta. Frankly, New York was the last of Destiny's concerns. She really liked Gregory and wanted to see where this relationship would go, and that meant she'd be crazy if she tried to fool herself into ignoring his mood this morning.

It has to have crossed his mind. How is this supposed to work between us while I transition or, for that matter, after. I know he's bi, but how does that work long-term for him with a trans woman?

"I smell something burning, girl. What's frying that brain of yours?"

"I was just thinking about Gregory. I'm really attracted to him. That man is the total package. But this has got to be the eye of the storm for him."

"Isn't the eye of the storm the calm part?"

"Yeah, but it's also the precursor to the violent winds coming. I mean, when he saw me on television, I was just another guy in drag. Then, we meet in person, and he finds out the guy is just the shell hiding the woman within."

Destiny started pulling on a lock of her hair, a habit she'd developed whenever she was nervous. "I mean, he's gone with me to my appointments and our time together has been amazing. But the thing is, I've had a lot of time to become who I am inside. The physical changes have been slow and steady. My family and close friends only began to notice six weeks ago. By that time, I'd been on hormones for a year and had begun prepping for surgery."

Alaska pulled the car into a parking space, and they exited the car.

"Gregory and I have only been together three weeks. He must have done some research because he's a masterful lover and asks questions rather than make a wrong move."

"So, just what is the problem? You said he's bi, so maybe he's just crazy about you enough to do what it takes." Anthony locked the car and they walked into the side door, dodging between the men that were dismantling and moving props and stage parts into a large truck. Once inside, the two friends separated and Destiny walked through the door of her private dressing room, designated for her as the star of the reunion.

"Hurry up, girl," admonished Anthony. "I'm starving and the special at Vincent's today is rib eye."

"Yeah, yeah. I'm moving." Destiny laughed as she turned on the lights and walked over to pack the makeup on her dressing table.

"Hello, Theodore." The voice was one Destiny would recognize in a room with an orchestra playing in her ears.

Reuben. Shit.

"H-how did you get in here? Why are you here?" Destiny pulled up every inner reserve she had. She was done being fearful of this bastard.

"Our relationship ended almost two months ago. I said everything I had to say then." At that point, Destiny made her first and final mistake. She turned her back on Reuben and went back to packing the things on her dressing table.

"Well, let me take you to lunch after you're done packing, then."

"I have plans for lunch and after that I have a doctor's appointment. I'm having my surgery next week."

Reuben had moved directly behind Destiny. In the mirror, she saw a look of rage like none Reuben had ever worn.

I need help. I wonder if Anthony can hear me.

Destiny opened her mouth to scream but before she could utter a sound, Reuben grabbed her by the throat and shoved a ball gag in her mouth, almost breaking her front teeth in the process.

Oh my God. He's going to kill me! Think, girl. This isn't ending well.

Concentration became impossible as fear infused every pore in Destiny's being. Reuben threw her body to the floor like a rag doll, and Destiny saw stars as her head hit the hard tile floor. Tears began to stream down her face as Reuben waved a knife in front of her.

"I've always given you everything you could ever need and many things you wanted. Well, bitch, you want to be a woman now? You don't need a doctor's appointment. I'm your surgeon, here to make your dreams come true."

Realization of what Reuben meant was the last conscious thought Destiny had. His fist slammed into her and the final thing she felt before she slipped into unconsciousness was a fiery pain in her groin. She screamed once more around the gag and then the world went black.

15

The room was silent except for the steady beep, beep, beep of the cardiac monitor showing heart rate and rhythm, blood pressure, respiratory rate, and oxygen saturation. Each reading was communicated by one of the multi-colored wires attached to the small figure in the bed. Nurses made their observations, documented their findings, and left as silently as they came.

In the center of the bed lay the semiconscious figure of Destiny Washington. She'd lain this way for hours. Her wounds were serious but not fatal. On the explicit telephone instructions of a Mrs. Laura Washington (who further demanded her daughter's name was Destiny, not Theodore), there was to be no surgery until she arrived and enlisted the consultation of Dr. Branson, Destiny's personal physician.

Outside the unit was a sterile room that held ten chairs and a television, with a door on one wall that led to a bathroom. Gregory sat forlornly in one chair with River at his feet. They wouldn't let him stay at Destiny's bedside and they wouldn't give him information. Apparently, boyfriends didn't qualify as family.

Before the day was over, the room would be filled to overflowing. The Sayville team, as Ron had labeled Destiny's family and friends, would be arriving any moment. For now, Bishop, Jordan, and Deejay sat with Gregory, supporting him in his silent vigil.

The wait had dragged on for hours and Gregory wanted to scream when detectives from the special victims unit that had been notified by the police who'd answered the 911 call showed up at the hospital and began to grill him about what happened. The saving grace had been someone named Anthony, also known as the drag queen Alaska, who stepped in and patiently answered the endless and repetitive questions fired at him.

Apparently, Reuben Bradshaw was pressing charges of assault. He didn't seem to think it was legal for Anthony to interfere when he was mutilating his "boyfriend" who seemed to desire gender reassignment. Said significant other was now lying in a critical-care bed recovering from the effects of Anthony "persuading" him to stop trying to kill Destiny.

Gregory stared out the lone window in the dismal green waiting room and tried hard to remain calm. *A seizure is the last thing anyone needs right now.* At that moment, River put both paws on his knees and laid his head on Gregory's lap. "Thanks, boy," Gregory said as he stroked the dog's curly hair. "Help me hold out."

Suddenly, there was a racket outside the door to the waiting room that could only mean one thing. "Finally!" exclaimed an exhausted Gregory. "Now we can get somewhere." Dale, EJ, Laura, and Nathan poured into the room, and Laura walked over to Gregory to hug him hard as he stood to greet her. "I'm so glad to see you," he said, shaking as she comforted him. He then turned and grabbed Alaska's hand. "This is someone you need to meet. He saved Destiny's life." He paused in the introductions. "Do you prefer Anthony or Alaska?"

"Just call me Alaska. I'm always on, whether I'm in drag or not."

Nathan and Laura took turns shaking Alaska's hand. "We'll never be able to thank you enough for being there for our girl," Laura said and then turned her attention back to Gregory.

"How are you doing? Have they let you see her?"

"No. They say I'm not family, so I've only been allowed a few moments here and there."

"Well, that's one of the first things we're gonna fix right now. That and the gender business. Let's go!"

Damn, this is not a woman you want to piss off. I feel sorry for the hospital staff.

Gregory wasted no time taking River's lead and following Laura Washington through the door. As they left the waiting room, he heard laughter when Nathan Washington said, "Strap in, folks. Typhoon Laura is headed east."

The unit was a U-shaped place with nursing stations at each end. Laura and Gregory approached the first station and she announced to the clerk, "I'm Destiny Washington's mother and I'd like to speak to your manager, please."

The clerk looked confused and began to deny the presence of such a patient. Fortunately, Destiny's nurse was at the station and interceded.

"Good afternoon, Mrs. Washington. I'm Tamika, Destiny's nurse this shift. She's in room 323 if you want to visit while I contact our manager." She then looked at Gregory and River. "I'm sorry, but this time is only for family."

"Well, that's great. Tell your manager that Destiny's

family will await them in the room." She then placed her arm around Gregory's shoulder and nudged him toward the door of 323. "I understand you folks have been less than inviting to my daughter's partner. That will certainly stop now."

Gregory quickly moved into Destiny's room. He hated scenes and Laura Washington was more intense than he was prepared to handle. As he entered, he saw Destiny slowly shaking her head.

"Oh my god, baby, are you awake?" Gregory bent over the bed railing in time to see Destiny slowly open her eyes. "Easy now. Wait, let me turn off the lights." Swiftly, he walked over to the switch by the door and turned the lights off. He was so excited that it was only an afterthought that made him pull the door open and shout, "She's awake!"

Apparently, the nurse manager and some other administrator had arrived, and he was interrupting a heavy conversation. The only one who looked satisfied was Laura, but Gregory had no patience for whatever pissing contest they were engaged in.

"Hey! Did you guys hear me? She's awake!" He then returned to Destiny's bedside. "Oh my god, baby, we've all been so worried."

"Gregory?" Destiny's voice was groggy and hoarse, but Gregory didn't care. She was awake and that was all that mattered. "Reuben. He's here. Get help, I'm hurt."

"Shhhh. You're in the hospital and Reuben is handcuffed to his hospital bed. Anthony saved your life."

"Anthony?"

"Alaska. She came in just as Reuben had cut off your jeans and explained he was performing an emergency vaginoplasty. Damn, that man is crazy."

"Pain, burning, between my legs."

"You better let me explain that, Gregory." Dr. Branson had entered the room, followed by the whole gang. Laura and EJ were the first to reach the bed while Alaska came up on the side next to Gregory.

"Damn, girl, you scared me near to death!" He bent over the rails and kissed Destiny lightly on the head. "I'm sorry I didn't get there to prevent all the damage. I promise you this. That bastard will be eating through a straw for a long time."

Laura looked up from hugging Destiny and said, "Yeah, well, he'll be using that straw while he becomes somebody's girlfriend in the Larimer County Jail."

"He doesn't bottom, ever." Destiny's speech was improving but still hazy.

"Hmph," said Laura. "There's a first time for everything. He'll learn."

EJ, finally able to reach Destiny, slipped a small envelope in her hand. "This kept me going when my days were rough. I'm passing it on to you. I love you, girl, and I'm going to kill that bastard."

Dale grabbed EJ and led him out of the room. "Come on. You've seen her awake. I think it's time for you to get some air."

"I need to speak to Destiny and Gregory alone right now, so I'm asking everyone to leave the room." Dr. Branson's tone brooked no argument.

Laura stood up straight, indignation written all over her face and in her rigid posture.

"Yes, Mom. This means you too. Some conversations have to be held without parents. This is one such conversation." He gently ushered everyone out of the door. Nathan Washington, who'd silently slipped into the room, waited until everyone was gone save himself, Dr. Branson, and Gregory. He walked up to the bed and placed one hand gently on the area of Destiny's chest. "You know I've not been the greatest fan of this decision strictly out of fear for your safety. So hear me when I say to you, make the decisions that will best give you what you want when all the drama is over, Ms. Washington."

Nathan straightened and his gaze became steely. "I want you to be at your most fabulous when you attend my trial. I'm gonna kill that motherfucker. I can't trust the courts. He has enough money to work his crazy ass through this slanted justice system and come out free on the other side." A tear slowly trickled down Nathan's face as he faced Dr. Branson.

"You do whatever she wants and needs. Whatever money she ain't got, I got." He walked toward the door, tears flowing freely. "Won't need it where I'm going cuz I don't smoke. Sure as God made green grass, I'm gonna kill that bastard." As he made his way to the waiting room, Destiny's father could be heard repeating over and over, "Imma kill him. Imma kill that bastard. Imma kill him."

16

Dr. Branson slowly pulled the covers back to reveal Destiny's injuries. "This is worse than I thought. A very angry person attacked you, Destiny."

Gregory stood against the wall. He didn't want to see. He didn't want to know. He wanted this to be a dream he'd wake up from.

"I know we originally planned for breast augmentation first, but this potentially changes things." Dr. Branson gently replaced the covers. "Suffice it to say, surgery Monday is off the table. I want you to have some time to heal and consider what your next steps are going to be."

"Okay, Dr. Branson, but nobody touches me except you. I didn't go through all I have to be hacked up by some stranger who has no idea who I am." Destiny's voice became stronger the longer she was awake.

Gregory was having a hard time absorbing all this. Some deranged asshat had mutilated her, and she and Dr. Branson were talking about it like she'd had her purse snatched and needed to decide whether to replace it with Gucci or Prada.

"Are you two for real?" He looked at Destiny. "You just woke up from a coma after being attacked by a deranged man who, when caught, simply said he was saving you the cost of surgery. This man almost took your life and you're acting like he merely stole your favorite pumps."

He then turned on the doctor. "This is a serious matter. I've spent enough time in group rooms to know you don't just calmly stroll back into life after that. How are you not addressing this? Do the letters PTSD mean nothing to you? I mean..."

"Gregory, stop! Please!" Destiny began to shake and cry. "You may have been in groups, but I lead those groups for a living, and the one thing I know is everything is on the table."

"Sweetheart, I agree with you. That's why I can't understand how you know this and yet act like it's just another day!" Destiny may have been talking calmly, but her body language was screaming. Even through the bruises, he could see her face drawing tight. Her posture was stiff as she pressed the control to raise the head of the bed.

Dr Branson seemed to notice also because he began speaking like he was trying to approach a cornered animal.

"Listen, Destiny, Gregory has a point. How about I get Janice down here and you two can talk some before we make any major decisions?"

Destiny looked from Dr. Branson to Gregory and, pinching her lips together, took a deep breath through her nose. "So how about this," she said tersely. "Both of you get the fuck out of my room! Tell my parents and whoever the hell else is out there that today just ain't the day. Tomorrow's not looking good either."

Destiny let the head of her bed down a bit, turned to her

side, and pulled the covers up under her chin. The signal was clear. She was done talking.

Gregory was speechless.

Goodbye, Dr. Jekyll. Hello, Miss Hyde.

He wrapped River's leash around his hand and left the room. When he got to the waiting room, he told everyone what had happened.

"She says go away, that today just ain't the day and tomorrow's not looking good either."

This was met by a chorus of *whats* and *whys* until Nathan Washington let out a shrill whistle calling for silence. "Everybody, sit the hell down and shut the fuck up. This has already been a hard day. We're travel-weary and our nerves are frazzled. My daughter just woke from a traumatic, life-threatening event."

Laura Washington rose, grabbing her purse as she stood. He reached out and grabbed her arm, effectively stopping her.

"Not now, Laura. Sometimes you have to see your child as an adult. You've done your momma bear thing and now you need to back down."

"Are you saying you think leaving her alone is the best idea? I've always been there for Destiny since we were kids," said EJ, sounding like he was about to blow a gasket. "I'm going in there to let her know her best friend is still her best friend and I've got her back."

Dale grabbed his husband and pulled him back into his seat. "You're not listening, Eduard. Nathan is trying to make a point if we'll all listen." The mood in the room changed immediately.

The dynamic in this group impressed and confused Gregory. *These people are speaking a whole internal language I have no understanding of. Dale, who almost never speaks, calls*

EJ Eduard and he settles down. Everybody else is backing off like someone just passed out Xanax.

Dale spoke again. "Nathan, are you saying we should all go to our hotels and homes for now? Shouldn't somebody go in there and try to talk to her? I mean, it's not healthy for her to sit there and stew in her emotions without someone who can answer her questions and support her."

"I agree," said Dr. Branson, who'd managed to enter the space unnoticed. "The thing is, while everyone in this room is a stakeholder in what happens to Destiny, only one of us is the appropriate person to go in now." He took a seat as he addressed the room. "I've been working with Destiny for over two years on this transition. She has gone through a lot of counseling and psychological preparation for a variety of social scenarios." He shook his head slowly. "We've discussed Reuben at length and never did the possibility of such a volatile response enter the conversation. In preparing for the surgery that was supposed to take place on Monday, I've had multiple conversations with the only person I think can do any good right now." He looked Gregory in the eyes. "That's you, sir."

Gregory almost fell out of his chair with surprise. "Me?!"

"No offense, Gregory, but you can't possibly have known Destiny long enough." EJ looked like he was about to boil over once again.

Gregory was quick to nod in agreement.

Dr. Branson put his hands up to quiet the room as Laura (*I'm her mother*) and EJ (*I'm her first and oldest friend*) took turns to defend their position in Destiny's life. "Actually," continued Dr. Branson. "You're both making my point." He turned his attention to Laura. "Yes, you're her mother. She came to you as a bouncing baby boy whom you loved and supported through his journey of self-discovery, and you've done a superior job. Would that all my patients had parents like you and Nathan."

He then moved to face EJ. "I understand that the two of you were inseparable until you joined the military, and Teddy was the person you turned to when life turned against you."

"I'm surprised to hear you deadname Destiny, doctor." Gregory didn't care how important and smart these people were. He wasn't standing for disrespect, whether Destiny could hear it or not.

"I'm sorry, Gregory, but I'm not deadnaming Destiny. I'm making a point." He stood and faced Gregory.

River had moved to place his head in Gregory's lap, making Gregory realize he needed to attempt to calm down. He slowly stroked his fingers through the curly locks and focused on his breathing like he'd been taught. *Now isn't the time to have a meltdown.*

"My point is," Dr. Branson continued, "the only person in this room who knows Destiny as who she is from day one of this phase of her transition is the person she chose to trust at such a fragile time. Taking nothing from you, Laura, or you, EJ, but that person became Gregory."

Gregory began to mentally review all the counseling sessions they'd been through, both individual and together. *He's right. This is where the rubber hits the road.* He stood, picked up River's leash, and headed for the door. "It was nice meeting y'all. I'll see you when she's ready to have company."

He didn't wait for responses as he walked with purpose out of the lounge and back into the ICU unit, then pushed open the door to Destiny's room.

"Hey, baby. I'm back and we need to talk."

17

Nestled in the Rocky Mountain foothills, just thirty-five miles north of Red Deer, Colorado, lies the Rocky Mountain Surgery Center. The only center of its kind in the United States, every possible service is provided for clients undergoing gender reassignment surgery. Doctors, nurses, lawyers, and psychiatrists form teams to ensure their patients leave with everything they need to restart life as their true selves.

Anyone on the road that quiet Wednesday morning would have watched the procession of cars turning off the highway onto a private mountain road and wondered what VIP was in their sleepy little town.

A small white ambulette carried the tiny figure of Destiny Washington, also known as the drag queen Phoenix, as well as her partner Gregory and his service dog, River. Behind them trailed the Washingtons, the Jackson-Chenaults, and every drag queen known to *Drag Star* history. The story of what Destiny had suffered at the hands of her ex had spread like wildfire through the drag community, and everyone was there to cheer her on.

After many consultations and additional psychiatric evaluations, Destiny had decided to follow the suggestion of Dr. Branson and have bottom surgery first. Reassignment was rarely done in this order, but Destiny was determined to not allow Reuben to become her tragedy. She always planned to have bottom surgery anyway, and the decision to reverse the order was still her choice.

The surgical team met her at the operating room entrance and, after several rounds of hugs, kisses, and *I love yous*, she was wheeled off to the operating suite while the family and entourage were escorted to a large room that had been set up once the center received notice of the large number of people accompanying Destiny.

Gregory addressed the group. "Listen, everyone. Destiny is going to be in surgery for at least somewhere between five and seven hours." He knew it could even be longer as the procedure had been made all the more difficult by the attack. "Vincent's has closed off the main dining room to give us a comfortable place to be together while we wait."

Laura was resistant. "I want to be right here when my child comes out of surgery. I'm not going anywhere." She planted herself in one of the chairs and wrapped her arms around the purse in her lap.

Gregory knew that look. She wasn't going anywhere until she was ready. He watched as Nathan took the seat next to his wife and began speaking to her softly. Gently, he took her hand as he spoke. She began to cry, and he pulled a handkerchief from his pocket to gently dab away the tears. The scene was sad and beautiful all at the same time.

Jordan approached him. "Hey, let's take Deejay and River out for a break while this bunch gets sorted."

Together, they walked out into the garden area where he

and Jordan had each waited when they accompanied Destiny to her preoperative appointments.

"How are you doing, Gregory?" Jordan led the way to a bench. "This has been a lot for such a new relationship." He shook his head slowly. "I don't know if I would have been able to be so steadfast."

"It has been a ride and having to deal with all the personalities in that waiting room has been wearing." He began to absently run his hands through River's hair. "What else am I gonna do? I know I sound like a dime-store novel right now, but I'm falling in love with her and if this is what it takes, I'm all in."

"Seven hours is a long time. I think we should go to Vincent's to get something to eat, but then I have just the place where the wait for you will be easier than dealing with that crowd."

Gregory considered Jordan's idea for a moment and then shook his head. "I don't know. Dr. Branson has to be able to reach me so we can't go out of cell range."

"No worries. I got you covered."

Just then the door to the garden space opened and Ron came through. "I've convinced everyone to go to Vincent's." He turned his attention to Jordan. "I know that look. I'll see you guys in a few hours. Drive safe." He turned and went back into the waiting area. Through the glass, Gregory could see everyone moving toward the exits.

Okay, now Gregory was really confused. "What's he talking about?"

"Ron and I have a cabin up in the hills," Jordan explained. "I go there when I need to put the world behind me for a minute and just breathe." He slapped Gregory on one thigh. "It's a great place to just be, especially when you're dealing with our kind of stress."

Jordan had been correct. The little rustic cabin turned out to be just the balm for Gregory's soul. They let the dogs loose to explore and be off duty for a few hours. It never failed to amaze Gregory how, even off duty, River always came to find him every so often as if to check up on him. At first, he and Jordan just sat in camp chairs near the fireplace, drinking the world's worst coffee. To Gregory, it was ambrosia. The room was a crisp kind of cold, but the fire made it tolerable. Best of all, Jordan didn't try to fill the time with idle chatter.

After a while, the two men and their dogs left the cabin and explored the surrounding area until they came upon a small clearing with a small burn pit sitting in its center.

Jordan pointed to the area. "I first came here to perform a forgiveness ritual my grandmother taught me." He picked up a small ball laying in the grass and threw it. Deejay immediately took off after it. River quickly followed.

"Now I come here whenever I need to connect spiritually and pray or meditate."

Gregory watched as Jordan started a small fire in the pit. Once it was going, he pulled down a duffle Gregory hadn't noticed hanging on a low branch of a nearby tree. He took out a couple heavy blankets and spread them on the ground.

"I'm gonna go find the dogs." He smirked a little. "Not that they're far. You sit here and hopefully find the peace I do." With that, he walked off whistling.

Gregory looked at the little setup. He had to agree, he needed the peace of the moment. So he fell to his knees and as his thoughts turned to the slight body laying miles away on an operating table, the tears he'd held all day began to fall. And for the first time since an IED hit his camp and sent him home clinging to life, Gregory Grayson prayed.

He was still there, on his knees, River lying beside him, when Jordan returned to say it was time to return to town.

The quiet ride to Vincent's was quick and in no time, Gregory and Jordan were walking through the main doors.

The sign on the entrance read "Closed For Private Family Event." Inside, the large-screen television played the episodes from Destiny's season of Drag Race. Buffet tables buckled under the weight of the food Kevin and Vincent had spent the night preparing.

The sight of the food made Gregory realize he'd not eaten at all during the day, and he set about making himself a plate that could feed a platoon.

After polishing off the entire serving, he fed River and took him out for a bathroom break. Just as he returned, Gregory's phone rang. It was Dr. Branson.

"She's out of surgery, Gregory, but not yet awake. Where are you?"

"We brought everyone to Vincent's to wait and have a meal." Gregory didn't want to discuss other people. "How is she? Did the surgery come out the way she wanted? When can I see her?"

"Slow down, Gregory. She is stable. The surgery was a success in spite of the damage done during her attack. Her healing time may be a little longer, but only time will tell."

"Thanks, Doc. I'll let everyone know. We'll be there shortly."

"Hold on, Gregory. Destiny is in no shape to entertain a mob. I'll allow you and her parents tonight. That's all for a few days."

Gregory agreed and went to find the Washingtons. He spotted Laura first, who apparently had noticed Gregory on the phone and was hovering close by.

"How is she?"

"She came through like the champion she is, but Dr. Branson is only allowing you, Mr. Washington, and me to see her tonight. EJ and Dale can maybe come tomorrow. Everyone else for sure has to wait a few days until he's certain she's doing as well as hoped."

EJ, Dale, and Nathan Washington approached and seemed to have heard the tail end of the conversation. "You guys go on up to the hospital. We'll stay here and advise the crowd," EJ said. "Give her my love and tell her we'll see her tomorrow."

"Well, that's settled," said Nathan. "Let's go. I need to see my daughter."

Gregory didn't realize how long and hard he'd been holding his breath until he let out a deep and very vocal sigh. "It's almost over."

"Not until that bastard goes to jail or I kill him," said Nathan. "But for tonight, I'll be satisfied that she's okay."

EPILOGUE

Nestled near the foothills, a few miles north of the Red Deer Veteran's Hospital, stood the newly constructed home of Second Chances. It was a beautiful building. A Zen feeling began in the lobby where a bas-relief of a snowcapped mountain range decorated the entire back wall. A waterfall flowed down and cascaded over the rocks to an aquarium built to appear as a stream below.

By the time Destiny had healed sufficiently to travel, she and Gregory had decided separation was not a part of their plans. She discussed her desire with Dale, who had the perfect solution. After contract discussions with Dr. Mason and the Veteran's Administration Department of Mental Health, Red Deer became the location for the new Colorado branch of Chances, aptly named Second Chances, with Destiny Washington at the helm as director.

Destiny had always loved the view from the bay window in Dale's office and had one installed in her office that faced the beautiful Rocky Mountains. It was awe-inspiring, especially in the winter when the mountains were capped with snow.

No one was more excited about the new facility than Dr. Mason. The number of veterans in need of mental health services had grown beyond the capacity of the VA's outpatient services, and Second Chances would be a godsend for the men and women who would otherwise have no place to go.

Destiny realized how fortunate she was to be able to afford the counseling services of the Rocky Mountain Surgery Center. There were transgender veterans out there who needed that help and would never be able to afford it. She made a point of ensuring that Dr. Mason knew Dr. Janice Taylor would be providing her services at low or no cost, depending on income.

She'd just finished the final walk-through when Gregory and River came through the front doors.

"How'd it go? Did you win your appeal? What did Kevin say?"

"Pump your brakes, girl." Gregory laughed as he waved a letter in his hand. "Seventy-five percent disability retroactive to my day of discharge and reimbursement for River's training. Damn, babe, I can afford to go back to school and finally get my degree in social work."

"That's amazing! Keep that up and I can quit and become a kept woman."

"Well, right now we need to get home and get changed for the finale, Your Majesty."

∼

"MY GOD, WHAT A YEAR!" Destiny stood in front of the mirror in her dressing room as Alaska helped her into her gown. For tonight, the signature fire tones were hanging in their closet in New York. Tonight's gown, sponsored by

House of Zeva, was a vision decorated with Swarovski crystals and Japanese Akoya pearls. The arrangement created a stunning fire and ice effect.

Settling the crown on her signature flaming red locks, Destiny caught her friend's eye in the mirror's reflection. "You saved my life, Alaska. I don't know if I'll ever be able to thank you enough."

"Okay, girl, none of that. Tonight, we crown the new queen, and you join the legacy club. I hear tell they had to set aside damn near ten rows for your family and friends."

"Yeah, well, blame Paula for having the finale back in Colorado. Gregory's group, the crowd from Vincent's, half the staff from the Rocky Mountain Surgery Center, and all my staff from Second Chances, not to mention my Sayville family." Destiny shrugged. "What can I say, I never do things by halves."

A stagehand appeared at the door. "That may be, but right now we need you ladies to take your positions in the wings."

Alaska was announced first and blew Destiny a kiss as she crossed the stage for her interview with Paula.

Finally, it was Destiny's turn. Music played as she moved onto the stage and took her farewell walk, waving and blowing kisses, even as she registered that something was out of sorts. She'd done a million of these pageants. The outgoing queen always took her farewell walk before the new queen was crowned. But there stood this year's winner, De-Luxe, smiling and looking resplendent, wearing her robe and crown.

When she moved back upstage, the first thing she noticed was Paula Blu standing instead of sitting on the interview couch. Next to her stood Alaska, grinning from ear to ear like the cat that ate the canary.

The music changed and played softly in the background as Paula explained, "Tonight, ladies and gentlemen, we have two reasons to celebrate. As some of you know, we almost lost Queen Destiny a year ago." The audience murmured at Paula's words, and she waited a moment for them to quiet again.

"We've spent the year showing our love for Queen Destiny, but there is one person who has something very important to say." She turned and signaled to the queens lined up on the far side of the stage. They parted and through the gap came Gregory and River.

"It's my pleasure to present to some and introduce to others, Gregory Grayson, the king of our queen's heart!"

Destiny was confused and Gregory looked nervous as he approached her and handed her a bouquet made of orange alstroemeria and mango calla lilies.

"What's going on?" she asked.

Gregory slowly removed a white box from his pocket and went down on one knee.

"Just one last question, Your Majesty."

ABOUT THE AUTHOR

Miski Harris was born and raised in NY with her younger siblings. She's a nurse and a veteran who raised five sons while traveling the world. When she sets her mind to achieve something, she's unstoppable.

Her two lifelong constants have been her faith and love of books. Reading is her mainstay, and she is rarely seen without her Nook which holds over 2,000 books. She loves to give the characters who reside in her imagination life and has begun to fulfill a desire to write books of her own. She published her first M/M romance novel after a close friend challenged her to join the National Novel Writing Month initiative. The result was the first draft of her book. Several edits later, Don't Ask Don't Tell: Book 1 made its debut on Amazon bookshelves. It has since been joined by Book 2: Collateral Damage, Cruise, Boy Overboard, and a few anthology novellas, and there's more to come.

When asked to describe her in one word, friends say fierce. A past commander defined her as a "tender warrior." Friends, patients, and strangers can always find a strong advocate in this woman who's not afraid to forge ahead or speak her mind.

Miski believes challenge defines worlds to conquer and lines to cross, love and faith are the most powerful forces in the universe, and the only thing hindering success is to fail to try. She invites you to join her in a world where love is second to nothing and life is the greatest adventure of all.

Miski lives in Prince Georges County, Maryland, with her two precocious cats: Freddie and Marshall.